By royal decree, Harlequin Presents is delighted to bring you THE ROYAL HOUSE OF NIROLI. Step into the glamorous, enticing world of the Nirolian Royal Family. As the king ails he must find an heir...each month an exciting new installment follows the epic search for the true Nirolian king. Eight heirs, eight romances, eight fantastic stories! Favorite author Penny Jordan starts this fabulous new series with *The Future King's Pregnant Mistress*. It's time for playboy Prince Marco Fierezza to claim his rightful place—on the throne! But what will the king-in-waiting do when he discovers his mistress is pregnant?

Plus, Lucy Monroe brings you the final part of her MEDITERRANEAN BRIDES duet, *Taken: The Spaniard's Virgin*, where Miguel takes Amber's innocence. There's another sexy Spaniard in Trish Morey's *The Spaniard's Blackmailed Bride*, when Blair is blackmailed into marriage but Diablo's touch sets her body on fire! In *Bought for the Greek's Bed* by Julia James, Theo demands his new bride also be his wife in the bedroom. In *The Greek Millionaire's Mistress* by Catherine Spencer, Gina Hudson goes to settle an old score in Athens, only to fall into the arms—and bed!—of a tycoon. *The Sicilian's Red-Hot Revenge* by Kate Walker has a handsome, fiery Italian who wants revenge, but what happens when he discovers he's going to be a father? In Annie West's *The Sheikh's Ransomed Bride*, powerful Sheikh Rafiq rescues Belle from rebels, only to demand marriage in return! And in Maggie Cox's *The Millionaire Boss's Baby*, a brooding boss's sensual seduction proves too good to resist. Enjoy!

Harlequin Presents®

GREEK TYCOONS

They're the men who have everything—
except brides...

Wealth, power, charm—
what else could a heart-stoppingly handsome
tycoon need? In the GREEK TYCOONS
miniseries you have already been introduced to
some gorgeous Greek multimillionaires who are
in need of wives.

Now it's the turn of talented Harlequin Presents
author Julia James, with her sensual romance
Bought for the Greek's Bed

This tycoon has met his match, and he's decided
he *has* to have her...*whatever* that takes!

Julia James

BOUGHT FOR THE GREEK'S BED

GREEK
TYCOONS

HARLEQUIN®

TORONTO • NEW YORK • LONDON
AMSTERDAM • PARIS • SYDNEY • HAMBURG
STOCKHOLM • ATHENS • TOKYO • MILAN • MADRID
PRAGUE • WARSAW • BUDAPEST • AUCKLAND

ISBN-13: 978-0-373-12645-3
ISBN-10:   0-373-12645-X

BOUGHT FOR THE GREEK'S BED

First North American Publication 2007.

www.eHarlequin.com

Printed in U.S.A.

All about the author...
Julia James

JULIA JAMES lives in England with her family. Harlequin® novels were the first "grown-up" books she read as a teenager, alongside Georgette Heyer and Daphne du Maurier, and she's been reading them ever since. Julia adores the British countryside—in all its seasons—and is fascinated by all things historical, from castles to cottages. She also has a special love for the Mediterranean—"the most perfect landscape after England!" She considers both ideal settings for romance stories! Since becoming a romance writer, she has, she says, had the great good fortune to start discovering the Caribbean as well and is happy to report that those magical, beautiful islands are also ideal settings for romance stories. "One of the best things about writing romance is that it gives you a great excuse to take holidays in fabulous places," says Julia. "All in the name of research, of course!"

Her first stab at novel-writing was Regency romances. "But, alas, no one wanted to publish them," she says. She put her writing aside until her family commitments were clear, and then renewed her love affair with contemporary romances. "My writing partner and I made a pact not to give up until we were published—and we both succeeded! Natasha Oakley writes for Mills & Boon® Tender Romance™, and we faithfully read each other's works-in-progress and give each other a lot of free advice and encouragement."

In between writing, Julia enjoys walking, gardening, needlework, baking "extremely gooey chocolate cakes" and trying to stay fit!

CHAPTER ONE

VICKY could hear her heels clacking on the marble floor of the vast atrium as she headed towards the reception desk, which was an island in the middle of an ocean of gleaming white and metallic grey. The whole interior screamed modernity—ironic, really, Vicky found herself thinking, as the man who ran this whole mega-corporate shebang was as antediluvian as a dinosaur. A big, vicious dinosaur that ripped your throat out with its talons, tore you limb from limb, and then went on its way, searching for other prey to dismember.

Walking into this dinosaur's cavern now made it all come rushing back. In her head she could again hear that deep, dangerously accented voice, carving into her with a cold, vicious fury that had stripped the flesh from her bones with savage economy. She could hear the words, too, ugly and foul, not caring how they slayed her, his fathomless eyes pools of loathing and—worse than loathing—contempt. Then, having verbally dismembered her, he had simply walked out of her life

She had not seen him since. And yet today, this morning, right now, she was going to walk up to that reception desk she could see coming closer and closer, walk up to that svelte, immaculate female sitting there watching her approach, and ask to see him.

She felt her throat spasm.

I can't do this! I can't.

Protest sliced in her head. But her nervous feet kept on walking, ringing on the marble. She had to do it. She'd tried everything else, and this was the only avenue left. Letters had been returned, all phone calls blocked, all e-mails deleted unread.

Theo Theakis had absolutely no intention of letting her get close enough to ask him for what she wanted.

Even as she replayed the thought in her mind, she felt a spurt of anger.

I shouldn't damn well have to go and ask him! It's not his to hand out or withhold. It's mine. Mine.

To her grim chagrin, however, the law did not see it that way. What she wanted was not, as her lawyer had sympathetically but regretfully informed her, hers to have, let alone dispose of.

'It requires Mr Theakis's consent,' her lawyer had repeated.

Her face darkened now as she closed in on the reception desk.

He's going to give me his damn consent, or I'm going to—

'May I help you?'

The receptionist's voice was light and impersonal. But her eyes had flicked over Vicky's outfit, and Vicky got the instant feeling that she had been classified precisely according to the cost of it. Well, her clothes at least should pass muster in these palatial corporate surroundings. Her suit might be well over a year out of date fashion-wise, but its designer label status was obvious to anyone with an eye for couture. Not that she herself had such an eye, but the world she'd once moved in—albeit so briefly—had been ruthlessly observant in that respect. And now this rare remnant of that vast wardrobe she had once had at her indifferent disposal was finally coming in useful. It was getting her the attentive focus of someone who was standing in the way of what she wanted.

'Thank you.' She smiled, striving to keep her voice just as

light and impersonal. It was hard, though, given the mixture of apprehension and anger that was biting away inside her. But, whatever the strength of her feelings about her situation, there wasn't the slightest point showing them now.

So she simply stood there, as poised as she could, knowing that the pale ice-blue dress and jacket she was wearing was perfectly cut, and that the thin silver necklace went with it flawlessly, as did her high-heeled shoes and handbag, which were both colour co-ordinated. Her hair, newly washed and styled—albeit by herself, not a top hairdresser—flicked neatly out at the ends, and was drawn off her forehead by a hairband the exact colour as the rest of her outfit. Her make-up was minimal and restrained, and the scent she was wearing was a classic fragrance she'd got as a free sample in a department store a while ago.

She looked, she knew, expensive, classic, English and—oh, dear God, please—sufficiently appropriate to get past this hurdle.

Right, time to do it—now.

In a deliberately poised voice, she spoke.

'I'd like to see Mr Theakis,' she said. She made her tones slightly more cultured than she usually bothered to do. But this was England, and these things counted. She gave the name as though it were something she did every day, as a matter of course. As if, equally as a matter of course, her giving it were not in the slightest exceptional and would always meet with compliance.

Was it going to happen now? She must not let any uncertainty show in her face.

'Whom shall I say?' the receptionist enquired. Vicky could tell that she was staying neutral at this point, but that she had conceded that it was indeed possible that this designer-dressed female might actually be someone allowed that level of access. Might even, unlikely though it was, given the restraint of her appearance, be a female granted the privilege of personal intimacy with Theo Theakis. But Vicky also knew, feeling another bite of her tightly leashed anger at having to be here at all, that she did not look nearly voluptuously delectable enough to be one of his legion of mistresses.

Vicky gave a small, poised smile.

'Mrs Theakis,' she said.

Theo Theakis sat back in his leather executive chair and felt his blood pressure spike. The phone he'd just picked up and discarded lay on the vast expanse of mahogany desk in front of him, as if it were contaminated.

And so it was.

She was here, downstairs, in this very building. *His* building. His London HQ. She had walked into *his* company, *his* territory, *daring* to do so! His eyes narrowed. Was she mad? Daring to come near him again after he'd thrown her from him like a diseased rag? She must be mad to be so stupid as to come within a hundred miles of him!

Or just shameless?

His face darkened. Shame was not a word she knew. Nor disgrace. Nor guilt.

No, she neither knew or felt any of those things. She'd done what she had done and had flaunted it, even thrown it in his face, and had felt nothing—nothing at all about it. No hesitation, no compunction, no remorse.

And now she had the effrontery to turn up and ask to see him. As though she had any right to do so. That woman had no rights to anything—let alone what he knew she was here for.

And certainly no right—his eyes flashed with a dangerous, dark anger that went deep to the heart of him—no right at all, to call herself what she still did...

His wife.

* * *

Vicky sat on one of the dark grey leather sofas that were arranged neatly around a smoked glass table. In front of her, laid out with pristine precision, were the day's leading newspapers in half a dozen languages. Including Greek. With a fragment of her brain that was still functioning normally she started to read the headline that was visible. Her Greek was rusty—she'd deliberately not used any of the language she'd acquired—and now her brain balked at forming sounds out of the alien writing. But at least it gave her mind something to do—something other than just going round and round in an ever-tightening loop.

I ought to just stand up and walk out. Not care that he's refused to see me. Not sit here like a lemon with some insane idea of doorstepping him when he leaves! Because he might not leave—he's got a flat here, somewhere up above his damn executive suite. And anyway the lift probably goes down to an underground car park, where he's either got one of his flash cars or a chauffeured limo waiting. There's no reason he should walk past me...

So she should go, she knew. It was pointless just continuing to sit here, with her stomach tying itself in knots and her feet slowly starting to ache in their unaccustomed high-heeled shoes.

But I want what I came for. I won't go back empty-handed until I've done everything I can to get it!

Determination gave strength to her expression. What she wanted was rightfully hers—and she'd been cheated of it. Cheated of what she had been promised—what she needed. Needed now, two years later, with imperative urgency. She could afford to wait no longer. She needed that money!

And it was that thought only that was keeping her glued to the grey leather as the slow minutes passed. Pointless, she half accepted, and yet the deep, deep sense of outrage she felt still kept her there.

She had sat for almost two hours before she finally accepted that she would have to throw in the towel this time around. Sinkingly resigned, Vicky knew that, stupid as she would look, she would just have to get to her feet and leave. People had been coming and going intermittently all the time, and she knew she'd been on the receiving end of some half-puzzled, half-assessing looks—not least by the receptionist. With a sense of bitter resignation she folded up the last of the newspapers and replaced it on the table. Useless—quite useless! She would just have to think of some other way of achieving her end. Quite what, though, she had no idea. She'd already done everything she could think of, including looking at the possibility of taking legal action, which had been promptly shot down by her lawyer. A face-to-face confrontation with her husband had been her last resort. Her eyes flashed darkly. Not surprisingly, considering that Theo Theakis was the last person on earth she ever wanted to see again!

Which was why, as she picked up her handbag from the floor and prepared to stand, bitter with defeat, her stomach suddenly plummeted right down to her heels. Right there in front of her appeared a bevy of suited figures, gracefully exiting one of the lifts and sweeping forwards across the marble floor to the revolving doors of the Theakis Corp's London HQ.

It was him.

She could see him. Her eyes went to him immediately, drawn by that malign awareness that had been like doom over her ever since that first fateful encounter. Half a head taller than the other suits around him, he strode forward, his pace faster than theirs, more impatient, as they hurried to keep up. One of the group was talking to him, his expression concentrated, and Theo had his face half turned towards the man.

Vicky felt herself go cold.

Oh, God, don't do this to me! Don't, please!

Because she could feel it again—feel that tremor in her

veins that Theo Theakis could always set running in her whenever she looked at him. It was as if she was mesmerised, like a rabbit seeing a fast car approaching and not being able to move, not being able to drag her eyes away.

She'd forgotten his impact, his raw physical force. It was not just his height, or the breadth of his shoulders and the leanness of his hips. It was not the fact that he looked like a billion dollars in a charcoal handmade suit that must have cost thousands of pounds, with his dark, sable hair immaculately styled, or that his face seemed as if it was planed from a fine-grained stone that revealed every perfect honed contour. It was more than that—it was his eyes, his dark, fathomless eyes, that could look at her with such coldness, with such savage fury, and with another expression that she would not, *would not*, let herself remember. Even now, when he wasn't even looking at her, when he was half focussed, clearly impatient, on what was being said to him. She saw him give a brief assenting nod, and look ahead again.

And that was when he saw her.

She could see it happening. See the precise moment when he registered her presence. See the initial flash of disbelief— followed by blinding fury.

And then it was gone. Just—gone. As she was gone from his vision. Gone from the slightest claim on the smallest portion of his attention. He had simply blanked her out as if she did not exist. As if she had not been sitting there for nearly two whole hours, waiting. Waiting for him to descend to ground level, where the mortals dwelt in their lowly places, far, far from the exclusively rich, powerful people that made up his world.

He was walking past her, still surrounded by his entourage. Any moment now he would be past the sofas and out of the sheer glass door, which one of the group was already hurrying to hold steady for his august passage. Very soon he would be out of the building he owned, the company he owned, and away from the people he owned.

She surged to her feet towards him.

She saw his head turn, just by a fraction. But not towards her. He gave one of the suits flanking the outer edge of his entourage an almost imperceptible shake of his head. Vicky saw the man peel off from the group, cross behind it with a swiftness that was as soft-footed as it was unanticipated by her, and intercept and block her path exactly where she would have been level with her target.

'Get out of my way!' It was a hiss of fury from her. It was like a spot of rain on a rock. The man didn't move.

'I'm sorry, miss,' he said. His eyes didn't meet hers, his body didn't touch hers—he just stood there, blocking her way. Letting Theo Theakis get away from her and stride off with total and complete unconcern for the fact that he had taken something from her that was not his to take and had kept it.

Her self-control was at breaking point. She could feel it snapping like a dry twig beneath her high heels. She felt her hand arch up, gripping the soft leather clutch bag she was holding like some kind of slingshot, and with every ounce of muscle in her arm she hurled it towards the man who was walking past her, walking out on her. Totally stonewalling her.

'Speak to me, you *bastard*! Damn well *speak* to me!'

The handbag bounced off one of the suits' shoulders, falling to the ground. The bodyguard in front of her caught her arm, too late to stop her impetuous action, but in time to force it down, not roughly, but with the strength his profession required of him.

'None of that, please,' he said, and there was a slight grimness to his mouth—presumably because, she thought, with a glance of vicious satisfaction, he hadn't expected a 'nice young Englishwoman' to behave in such an outrageous fashion.

Not that it had done her the slightest good at all. The entourage just kept going—hastened, even. Though the man at the centre did not change his pace by a centimetre. He simply walked out of the building and disappeared into the sleek black limo that was waiting at the kerb. The car moved off. He had gone.

You swine, thought Vicky, trembling all over. You absolute, total swine.

She had never, ever hated him so much as at that moment.

Theo let his gaze rest silently, impassively, on the newspaper clipping that had been placed in front of him. He was at breakfast in his London apartment, and on the other side of the table his private secretary stood, uneasily waiting for his employer's reaction. It would not be good, Demetrious knew. Theo Theakis hated anything about his private life getting into the press— which was ironic, really, since the life he led made the press very interested in him indeed, even though they could never get much information on him at all.

Theo Theakis managed his privacy ruthlessly. Even when the press could smell a really juicy story bubbling beneath the expensive surface of his tycoon's existence, Theo would remain calm. Eighteen months ago, when rumours had started to circulate like buzzing wasps about just why his apparently unexceptional marriage had proved so exceptionally brief, the press had been hot on his tail. But, as usual, they'd got absolutely nothing beyond the bland statement issued at Theo Theakis's curt instruction. Which was exactly why, Demetrious knew with a sinking heart, the tabloid from which the cutting had been taken had snapped up this latest little morsel.

He stood now, watching and waiting for his employer's reaction. He wouldn't show much, Demetrious knew, but he was aware that the mask of impassivity would be just that—a mask. Demetrious was grateful for it. Without the mask he would probably have been blasted to stone already by now.

For a few seconds there was silence. At least, thought Demetrious gratefully, there was no picture to go with the newspaper article. What had happened yesterday in Theakis HQ would have made a photo opportunity for any paparazzi to die for. As it was, it was nothing more than a coyly worded few paragraphs, laced with speculation, about just what had caused the former Mrs Theo Theakis to hurl her handbag at him and call him an unbecoming name. The journalist in question had teamed the article with an old photograph from the press archives of Theo Theakis, looking svelte in a tux, walking into some top hotel in Athens with a blonde, English, couture-dressed woman on his arm. Her expression was as impassive as his employer's was now.

But she certainly hadn't been impassive yesterday. And nothing could hide the glee with which the brief, gossipy article had been written up.

Theo Theakis's eyes snapped up.

'Find out who talked to these parasites and then sack them,' he said.

Then he went on with his breakfast.

Demetrious stood back. The man was ruthless, all right. There were times, definitely, when he felt sorry for anyone who ever got on the wrong side of Theo Theakis. Like his ex-wife. Demetrious wondered why she'd done what she had. Surely by now she must know it was just a waste of her time? She'd been plaguing his boss for weeks now, and he'd not given an inch. He wasn't going to, either. Demetrious could tell. Whatever it was she so badly wanted, she could forget it! As far as Theo Theakis was concerned she clearly no longer existed.

Demetrious turned to go. He'd been dismissed, he knew, and sent on an errand he would not enjoy, but which had to be done all the same.

'One more thing—'

The deep voice halted him. Demetrious paused expectantly. Dark eyes looked at him with the same chilling impassivity.

'Instruct Mrs Theakis to be here tonight at eight-thirty,' said his employer.

CHAPTER TWO

VICKY was ploughing through paperwork. There was a never-ending stream of it: forms in triplicate, and worse, letters of application, case notes, invoices, accounts and any number of records, listings and statistical analyses. But it all had to be done, however frustrating. It was the only way, Vicky knew, to achieve what this small voluntary group, Freshstart, was dedicated to achieving—making some attempt to catch those children who were slipping through the education net and who needed the kind of dedicated, intensive, out-of-school catch-up tutoring that the organisation sought to provide them with.

Money was, of course, their perpetual challenge. For every pound the group had, it could easily have spent five times that amount, and the number of children who needed its services was not diminishing.

She gave a sharp sigh of frustration, which intensified as she picked up the next folder—the batch of quotes from West Country building firms for doing up Jem's house. Jem had deliberately kept the work to the barest minimum—a new roof, new electrics, new flooring—to secure the property and make it comply with Health and Safety regulations. Everything else they would have to do themselves—painting, decorating, furnishing—even if they had to beg, borrow or steal. But the main

structural and safety work just had to be done professionally—
and it was going to cost a fortune.

Yet the house, Pycott Grange, was a godsend. Jem had inherited it the previous year from his childless maternal great-
uncle, and now that probate had been granted he could take
occupation. Although it was very run down, after years of
neglect, it had two outstanding advantages: it was large,
standing in its own generous grounds, and it was close to the
Devonshire seaside. Both those conditions made it ideal for
what everyone hoped would be Freshstart's latest venture. So
many of the children it helped came from backgrounds that
were grim in the extreme—deprived, dysfunctional families,
trapped in dreary inner-city environments that simply rein-
forced all their educational problems. But if some of those
children could just get a break, right away from their normal
bleak lives, it might provide the catalyst they needed to see
school as a vital ladder they could climb to get out of the conditions they'd been born into rather than the enemy. Two weeks
at the Grange, with a mix of intensive tuition and space to play
sport and surf, might just succeed in turning their heads around,
giving them something to aim for in life other than the deadbeat
fate that inevitably awaited them.

But the Grange was going to cost a lot of money to be made
suitable for housing staff and pupils, and a lot more to run, as
well, before Jem's dream finally came true. Disappointment bit
into Vicky again. If the building work could start, without more
delay, then there was a really good prospect that the Grange
could open its doors in time for the long school summer
holidays coming up in a few months. Already Freshstart had a
list as long as your arm of children they would like to recom-
mend for the experience. But without cash the Grange would
continue to crumble away, unused and unusable.

If we just had the money, she thought. Right now. And they

should have the money. That was the most galling part of it. They *should*—it was there, sitting uselessly in a bank account, ready to be used. Except that—

I want what's mine!

Anger injected itself into the frustration. *It's mine—I was promised it. It was part of that damned devil's agreement I made—the one I knew I shouldn't have made, but I did, all the same. Because I felt...*

She paused mentally, then finished the sentence. Felt obligated.

Wretchedness twisted inside her as painful memories came flooding back.

Vicky could hardly remember her father. She had always known that he had been born to riches, but to Andreas Fournatos his money was no more than a tool. At an early age he had taken his share of his patrimony and gone to work for an international aid agency, where he had met her mother and married her—only to die tragically when Vicky was not yet five. It had been his money, inherited by his widow, which had set up Freshstart, and Vicky's mother had run the organisation until Vicky had taken over her role.

She had had very little contact with her father's side of the family—except for her one uncle. Despite hardly knowing her, Aristides Fournatos had been so good to her, so incredibly kind and welcoming. She had always understood why her mother had withdrawn from her late husband's family all those years ago—because it had simply hurt too much to be reminded of the man she had married and lost so early. So, although there had been Christmas cards and birthday presents arriving regularly for Vicky throughout her childhood from her Greek uncle, her mother had never wanted to return to Greece, and had never wanted Vicky to accept her uncle's invitations.

Aristides had respected her mother's wishes, knowing how much it pained his sister-in-law to remember her first husband after his premature death. And when Vicky's mother had remarried, Aristides had been the first to congratulate her, accepting that she wanted to put all her emotional focus on her second husband—a divorced teacher with a son the same age as Vicky—and raise Vicky to be English, with Geoff as the only father she could remember. They had been a happy, close-knit family, living an ordinary, middle class life.

But when Vicky had been finishing her university course Geoff had been given the opportunity to participate in a teaching exchange in Australia. He and her mother had moved there, finding both the job and the lifestyle so congenial that they had decided to stay. Vicky could not have been more pleased for them, but, adult though she was, she'd still felt miserable and lonely, left behind in England.

That was when her uncle Aristides had suddenly swept back into her life. He had descended on Vicky and carried her off to Greece for a much needed holiday and a change of scene. And also for him to get to know his niece better. His arrival had had her mother's blessing—she had accepted that it was only natural that her daughter should get to know, even if belatedly, her own father's family, and now that she had emigrated to Australia she was beyond the painful associations herself.

Having been brought up in England, in an English family, it had been strange for Vicky to realise that she was, by birth, half-Greek. But far, far more alien than coming to terms with the cultural heritage she had never known had been coming to terms with another aspect of her paternal family. Its wealth.

Because her father's money had been spent on charitable causes, she had never really registered just how very different the lifestyle of her uncle would be. But staying with Aristides in Greece had opened her eyes, and she had been unable to help feeling how unreal his wealthy lifestyle was compared to her own. For all his wealth, however, her uncle was warm, and kind, and had embraced her wholeheartedly as his brother's child. A widower in late middle age, without children, he was, Vicky had seen with fondness, clearly set on lavishing on her all the pampering that he would have bestowed on a daughter of his own. While honouring his brother's altruism, and accepting her mother's desire to put the tragic past behind her, Aristides had nevertheless made no bones about wanting to make up for what he considered his niece's material deprivation.

At first Vicky had tried to stop him lavishing his money on her, but then, seeing him so obviously hurt by her refusal to let him buy her the beautiful clothes that he'd wanted her to have, she'd given gave in. After all, it was only a holiday. Not real life. So she'd stopped refusing and had let herself be pampered. Her uncle had taken so much pleasure in doing so.

'Andreas would be so proud of you! So proud! His so-beautiful daughter!' he would say, time and again, with a tear openly in his eye, his emotion unashamedly apparent and, Vicky had found with a smile, so very Greek.

And so very Greek, too, she'd discovered, in his attitude to young women of her age. They were, she'd had to accept, though loved to pieces, treated like beautiful ornamental dolls who must and should be petted and pampered, but also sheltered from the real world.

It had been the same when she'd made her second visit to Greece. She had visited her mother and stepfather in Australia for Christmas the previous year, and Aristides had invited her to spend the next festive season with him in Athens. But that time as soon as he'd greeted her she'd been able to tell something was wrong. There had been a strain about him that she'd sensed immediately.

Not that Aristides had said anything to her when she'd arrived in Athens. He'd simply reverted to his cosseting of her, telling her she was too thin and working too hard, she needed a holiday, some fun, new clothes. Because she'd known that his concern was genuine, and that he took great pleasure in pampering her, she'd once again given herself to his unreal world, where all the women wore couture clothes which they changed several times a day, according to the social function they were attending next. As before, she had gone along with it—because she'd seen the pleasure it gave her uncle to show off his young half-English niece, whose natural beauty was enhanced by clothes and jewellery.

'My late brother's daughter, Victoria,' he would introduce her, and she'd heard the pride in his voice as he did so, the affection, too. Family, she'd swiftly learnt, was of paramount importance in Greece.

For Vicky it had been fascinating, the glittering world she had dipped her toes into, where breathtaking consumption was the order of the day. Sitting around her uncle's vast dining room table, laden with crystal and silverware, with the female guests glittering like peacocks in their evening gowns and jewels, and the men as smart as magpies in their black-and-white tuxedos, she'd found herself realising with a strange curiosity that, had her father not been so determined to abnegate his wealthy background, this could have been her natural environment. Except, of course, she'd amended, she would not have had her English upbringing but one decidedly Greek. It had been a strange thought.

But she'd known that, fascinating as it was to observe this rarefied social milieu, it was, all the same, profoundly alien. She'd felt as if she was at a zoo, observing exotic mammals that lived lives of display and ostentation that were nothing to do with reality. Their biggest challenge would be which new yacht to buy, which designer to favour, or which Swiss bank to keep their private accounts in.

Not that their wealth made them horrible people—her uncle

was kindness personified, and everyone she'd met so far had been gracious and charming and easy to talk to.

All except one.

Vicky's expression took on a momentary darkening look.

She hadn't caught his name as her uncle had brought him over to be introduced to her before dinner, because as she'd turned to bestow a social smile on him it had suddenly frozen on her mouth. She'd felt her stomach turn slowly over.

Greek men were not tall. She'd got used to that now. But this man was tall. Six foot easily. Tall, and lean, and so devastatingly good-looking that her breath had congealed in her lungs as she'd stared at him, taking in sable hair, a hard-planed face already in its thirties, a blade of a nose, sculpted mouth and eyes—oh, eyes that were black as sloes. But with something hidden in them...

She'd forcibly made herself exhale and widen her smile. But it had been hard. She'd still felt frozen all over. Except for her pulse, which had suddenly surged in her veins. Mechanically she'd held out her hand in response to the introduction, and felt it taken by strong fingers and a wide palm. The contact had been brief, completely formal, and yet it had felt suddenly, out of nowhere, quite different. She'd withdrawn her hand as swiftly as politeness permitted.

'How do you do?' she said, wondering just what his name was. She'd missed her uncle saying it.

'Thespinis Fournatos,' the man acknowledged.

She was getting used to being addressed by her birth father's name. At home she'd taken Geoff's surname, because when her mother had married him he'd adopted her, and it was easier for them all to have the same surname. But understandably, she knew, her uncle thought of her as his brother's son, and to him she was Victoria Fournatos, not Vicky Peters.

But there was something about the way this man pronounced

her Greek name that sent a little shiver down her spine. Or maybe it was just because of the low timbre of his voice. The low, sexy timbre…

Because this man, she realised, with another surge of her pulse, was an incredibly attractive male. Whatever it was about the arrangement of his limbs and features, he had it—in buckets.

And he knew it, too.

She felt the tiny shiver turn from one of awareness to one of resistance. It wasn't that he was looking at her in any kind of suggestive way. It was more, she could tell, that he was perfectly used to women reacting to him the way that she had. So used to that reaction, in fact, that he took it for granted. Instantly she schooled herself against him, making herself ignore the breathless fluttering in her insides. Instead, she glanced at her uncle, who made some remark to the man in Greek, which Vicky did not understand. She knew a few Greek phrases, and a smattering of vocabulary, and was with practice and effort just about able to read Greek script haltingly, but rapid speech was completely beyond her.

'You live in England, I believe, Thespinis Fournatos?' The man turned his attention to her, with the slightest query in his voice. More than a query, thought Vicky—almost disapproval.

'Yes,' she said, leaving it at that. 'My uncle very kindly invited me for Christmas. However, I understand that in Greece Easter is the most important time of the year—a much more significant event than Christmas in the calendar.'

'Indeed,' he returned, and for a few minutes they engaged, with Aristides, in a brief conversation about seasonal celebrations.

It was quite an innocuous conversation, and yet Vicky was glad when it finished—glad when a highly polished, dramatically beautiful woman, a good few years older than herself, came gliding up to them and greeted the tall man with a low and clearly enthusiastic husk in her voice. She spoke Greek fluently, and made no attempt to recognise Vicky's presence.

Although Vicky could sense that Aristides was annoyed by the interruption, she herself took the opportunity to murmur, 'Do please excuse me,' and glided off to talk to some of her uncle's other guests.

She was equally relieved when the seating arrangements at dinner put her at the other end of the table, away from the man with the devastating looks and the disturbing presence. The Greek woman who had accosted him was seated beside him, Vicky saw, and she was glad of it. Yet for all the woman's obvious intention to keep the man's attention turned firmly on herself for the duration, Vicky was sure that every now and then those sloe-dark eyes would turn in her direction.

She didn't like it. There was something that disturbed her at the thought of that tall, dark and leanly compelling man looking at her. She could feel it in the tensing of her body.

Why was she reacting like this? she interrogated herself bracingly. She knew she was physically attractive, had learnt to cope with male attention, so why was this man able to make her feel so self-conscious? As if she were a schoolgirl, not a grown woman of twenty-four.

And why did she get the uncomfortable feeling that he was assessing her, observing her? It wasn't, she knew, that he was eying her up—though if he had been she would not have liked that in the slightest. Maybe, she chivvied herself, she was just imagining things. When his dark eyes intercepted hers it was nothing more than a trick of her line of sight, of her being so irritatingly aware of him. An awareness that only increased during the meal, along with her discomfort.

It was as the guests were finally leaving, late into the night, that the tall man whose name she had not caught came up to her. His dinner jacket, she noted abstractedly, sat across his shoulders to perfection, honing down to lean hips and long legs. Again she felt that irritating flurry of awareness and was annoyed by it. There was something unnerving about the man, and she didn't like it.

'Good night, Thespinis Fournatos,' he said, and looked down at her a moment. There was a look in his eyes that this time she could not mistake. It was definitely an assessing look.

Her back stiffened, even as her pulse gave a sudden little jump.

'Good night,' she replied, her voice as formal as she could make it. As indifferent as she could get away with. She turned to bid good night to another departing guest.

Afterwards, when everyone was gone, her uncle loosened his bow tie and top shirt button, poured himself another brandy from the liqueur tray, and said to her, in a very casual voice, 'What did you think of him?'

'Who?' said Vicky, automatically starting to pile up the coffee cups, even though she knew a bevy of maids would appear to clear away the mess the moment she and her uncle retired.

'Our handsome guest,' answered her uncle.

Vicky did not need to ask who he meant.

'Very handsome indeed,' she said, as neutrally as possible.

Her uncle seemed pleased with her reply.

'He's invited us for lunch at the yacht club tomorrow,' he informed her. 'It's a very popular place—you'll like it. It's at Piraeus.'

I might like it more without Mr Handsome there, she thought. But she did not say it. Still, it was a place she had not seen yet—Piraeus, the port of Athens. But, instead of saying anything more on that, she found herself changing the subject.

'Uncle, is everything all right?'

The enquiry had come out of nowhere, but it had been triggered by a sudden recognition that, despite the smile on her uncle's face, there was tension in it, too—a tension that had been masked during the evening but which was now, given the late hour, definitely visible.

But a hearty smile banished any tension about him.

'All right?' he riposted, rallying. 'Of course! Never better! Now, *pethi mou*, it is time for your bed, or you will have dark circles under your eyes to mar your beauty. And we cannot have that—we cannot have that at all!' He gave a sorrowing sigh. 'That Andreas were still alive to see how beautiful his daughter is! But I shall take care of you for him. That I promise you. And now to bed with you!'

He shooed her out, and she went, though she was still uneasy. Had she just been got rid of to stop her asking another question in that line of enquiry?

Yet the following day there was no sign of the tension she thought she'd seen in him, and when they arrived at the prestigious yacht club, clearly the preserve of the extremely well-heeled of Athens, her uncle's spirits were high. Hers were less so, and she found her reserve growing as the tall figure at the table they were being conducted to unfolded his lean frame and stood up.

Lunch was not a comfortable meal. Though the majority of the conversation was in English, Vicky got the feeling that another conversation was taking place—one that she was not a party to. But that was not the source of her discomfort. It was very much the man they were lunching with, and the way his dark, assessing eyes would flick to her every now and then, with a look in them that did not do her ease any good at all.

As the meal progressed she realised she was becoming increasingly aware of him—of his sheer physical presence, the way his hands moved, the strength of his fingers as they lifted a wineglass, or curved around the handle of his knife. The way his sable hair feathered very slightly over his forehead, the way the strong column of his throat moved as he talked. And the way he talked, whether in English or Greek, that low, resonant timbre doing strange things to her—things she would prefer not to happen. Such as raising her heart rate slightly, and making her stomach nip every now and then as her eyes, as they must during conversation, went to his face.

She watched covertly as he lifted his hand in the briefest gesture, to summon the *maître d'*. He came at once, instantly, and was immediately all attention. And Vicky realised, with a disturbing little frisson down her spine, that there was another reason other than his dark, planed looks that made him attractive.

It was the air of power that radiated from him. Not obvious, not ostentatious, not deliberate, but just—there.

This was a man who got what he wanted, and there would never, in his mind, be the slightest reason to think otherwise.

She gave an inward shiver. It wasn't right, her rational mind told her, to find that idea of uncompromising power adding to his masculinity. It was wrong for a host of reasons, ethical and moral.

But it was so, all the same.

And she resented it. Resented the man who made her think that way. Respond to him that way.

No! This was ridiculous. She was getting all worked up over someone who was, in the great scheme of things, completely irrelevant to her. He had invited her uncle for lunch, presumably for that singular mix of business and sociality that those in these wealthy circles practised as a matter of course, and she had been included in the invitation for no other reason than common courtesy.

She forced herself to relax. Her uncle was turning to her, saying something, and she made herself pay attention with a smile.

'You are fond of Mozart, are you not, *pethi mou*?'

She blinked. Where had that question come from? Nevertheless, she answered with a smile, 'Yes—why do you ask?'

But it was their host who answered.

'The Philharmonia are in Athens at the moment, and

tomorrow night they are giving a Mozart concert. Perhaps you would like to attend?'

Vicky's eyes went to her uncle. He was smiling at her benignly. She was confused. Did he want to go? If he did, she would be happy—more than happy—to go with him. Aristides liked showing her off, she knew, and as she did indeed like Mozart's music, she'd be happy to go to a concert.

'That sounds lovely,' she answered politely.

Her uncle's smile widened. 'Good, good.' He nodded. He glanced across at their host and said something in Greek that Vicky did not understand, and was answered briefly in the same language. He turned back to his niece.

'You can be ready by seven, can you not?' he asked.

'Yes, of course,' she answered. She frowned slightly. Why had her uncle spoken to their host about it?

She discovered, with a little stab of dismay, just why on her way back to Athens with Aristides.

'*He* wants to take me to the concert? But I thought we were going?'

'No, no,' said Aristides airily. 'Alas, I don't have time to go to concerts.'

But *he* does, thought Vicky. A strange sensation had settled over her and she didn't like it. She also didn't like the feeling that she had been stitched up—set up…

With no room to manoeuvre.

Well, she thought grimly now, that was how it had started— and how it had gone on. And even now, after everything that had happened, all the storm and stress, the rage and frustration, she still did not know how it had ended up the way it had. How she had gone from being escorted to a Mozart concert by a man whose company disturbed her so profoundly, to becoming—her mouth pressed together in a thin, self-condemning line—his wife.

Mrs Theo Theakis.

CHAPTER THREE

How could I have done it?

The question still burned in her head, just as it always had. How could she have gone and married Theo Theakis? She'd done it, in the end, for the best of reasons—and it had been the worst mistake of her life.

She could still remember the moment when her uncle had dropped the thunderbolt at her feet. Informing her that Theo Theakis was requesting her hand in marriage, as if they were living in the middle of a Victorian novel.

Aristides had beamed at her. 'Every woman in Athens wants to marry him!'

Well, every woman in Athens is welcome to him! thought Vicky, as she sat there, staring blankly at her uncle, disbelief taking over completely as he extolled the virtues of a man she barely knew—but knew enough to be very, very wary of. Since the Mozart concert she had seen Theo Theakis only a handful of times—and she could hardly have said he'd singled her out in any particular way. Apart from knowing that he was rich, disturbingly attractive, and, from the few conversations she'd had with him about any non-trivial subject, dauntingly and incisively intelligent, he was a complete stranger. Nothing more than an acquaintance of her uncle, and no one she wanted to get any closer to.

In fact, he was someone, for all the reasons she was so disturbingly aware of, her preferred option would have been to avoid. It would have been much, much safer...

And now, out of nowhere, her uncle was saying he wanted to *marry* her?

It was unbelievable—quite, quite unbelievable.

She wanted to laugh out loud at the absurdity of it, but as she stared at her uncle blindly she started to become aware of something behind the enthusiastic words. Something that dismayed her.

He was serious—he was really, really serious. And more than serious.

Vicky's heart chilled.

In her uncle's face was the same tension she'd seen when she'd arrived in Athens. The tension that she'd been moved to ask about the evening she'd met Theo Theakis for the first time. And something more than tension—fear.

It was shadowing his eyes, behind the eager smiles and the enthusiastic extolling of just why it would be so wonderful for her to be Mrs Theo Theakis. Behind her uncle's glowing verbiage of how every woman would envy her for having Theo Theakis as a husband, she could hear a much more prosaic message.

A dynastic marriage. Something quite unexceptional in the circles her uncle and aspiring bridegroom moved in. A marriage to link two wealthy families, two prominent Greek corporations.

Oh, Aristides did not say it like that—he used terms like 'so very suitable'—but Vicky could hear it all the same. And more. Vicky realised, with a sinking of her heart, that she could hear something much more anxious. Her uncle didn't just *want* her to marry Theo Theakis—he *needed* her to...

The chill around her heart intensified.

She waited, feeling her nerves biting, until he had finally finished his peroration, and was looking at her with an anticipation that was not just hopeful but fearful, too. She picked her words with extreme care.

'Uncle, would such a marriage be advantageous to you from a…a business point of view?'

There was a flicker in Aristides's eyes, and for a moment he looked hunted. Then he rallied, using the same tone of voice as he had when she had impulsively asked him whether everything was all right.

'Well, as you know, sadly my wife was not blessed with children, and so it has always been a question—what will happen to Fournatos when I am gone? Knowing that you, my niece, are married to Theo Theakis—whose business interests do not run contrary to those of Fournatos—would answer that question.'

Vicky frowned slightly. 'Does that mean the two companies would merge?'

A shuttered, almost evasive look came into Aristides' face.

'Perhaps, perhaps. Eventually. But—' His tone changed, becoming bright, eager, and, Vicky could tell from familiarity, deliberately pitched to address a female of her age, who should not be concerning herself with such mundane things as corporate mergers. 'This is not what a young woman thinks about when a man wants to marry her! And certainly not when the man is as handsome as Theo Theakis!'

It was the signal that he would not be drawn any more from the fairy tale he was spinning for her in such glowing colours. Vicky could get no more out of her uncle regarding the real reason behind this unbelievable idea of Theo Theakis saying he wanted to marry her. It was only the anxiety she felt about what she had seen so briefly in her uncle's face and respect for his kindness and generosity that stopped her telling him that she had never heard anything so absurd and walking straight out.

With rigid self-control she managed to hear him out, and

then, with all the verbal dexterity she could muster, she said, 'I'm…I'm overwhelmed.'

'Of course, of course!' Aristides said hurriedly. 'Such a wonderful thing is most momentous!'

Vicky hung on to her self-control by a thread. Groping about for some excuse to go, she muttered something about a dress fitting she had to get to in the city and slipped out of the room. Her mind was in turmoil.

What on *earth* was going on?

Her mouth set. Her uncle might not give her any answers, but she knew someone who could.

Even though he was the very last person she wanted to go and see.

She made herself do it, though. She went and confronted her suitor.

He did not seem surprised to see her. He received her in his executive suite in a gleaming new office block, getting up from a huge leather chair behind an even bigger desk. As he got to his feet, his business suit looking like a million euros all on its own, Vicky again felt that frisson go through her. Here, in his own corporate eyrie, the impression of power that emanated from him was more marked than ever.

She braced her shoulders. Well, that was all to the good. Obviously sentiment—despite her uncle's fairy-tale ramblings about how wonderful it would be for her to be married to so handsome and eligible a man as Theo Theakis—had nothing to do with why the man standing in front of her had informed Aristides Fournatos that he would be interested in marrying her.

Even as she formed the thought in her head, she had to cut it out straight away. 'Marriage' and 'Theo Theakis' in one sentence was an oxymoron of the highest order.

'Won't you sit down?'

The dark-timbred voice sent its usual uneasy frisson down her spine. She wished it wouldn't do that. She also wished she wasn't so ludicrously responsive to the damn man the whole time. It had been the same all the way through that Mozart concert he'd taken her to, when she'd sat in constrained silence during the music and made even more constrained small talk during the interval. She'd been dreading he'd suggest going for supper afterwards, and had been thankful that he had simply returned her back to her uncle's house, bidding her a formal good night. Since then she'd seen him a handful of times more, each encounter increasing her annoying awareness of his masculinity. His company disturbed her, and she kept out of any conversation that included him as much as possible. She also did her best to ignore the speculative looks and murmurs that she realised were directed towards them whenever they were together.

Now, of course, she knew just what they had been speculating about.

Well, it was time to put a stop to this nonsense right away.

She sat herself down in the chair Theo Theakis was indicating, just in front of his desk, and crossed her legs, suddenly wishing the skirt she had on was longer and looser.

'I take it your uncle has spoken to you?'

Her eyes went to him. His face was impassive as he took his seat again, but his eyes seemed watchful.

Vicky nodded. She took a breath.

'I don't mean to be rude,' she began, and saw the slightest gleam start in the dark eyes. 'But what on earth is going on?' She eyed him frankly; it seemed the best thing to do. It took more energy than she liked.

He studied her a moment, as if assessing her, and she found it took even more effort to hold his gaze. Then, after what seemed like an age, he spoke.

'If you were completely Greek, or had been brought up here, you would not be asking that question.' He quirked one eyebrow with a sardonic gesture. 'You would not, of course, even be here, at this moment, alone with me in my office. But I appreciate I must make allowances for your circumstances.'

Automatically Vicky could feel her hackles start to bristle, but he went smoothly on, leaning back in his imposing leather chair.

'Very well, let me explain to you just what, as you say, is going on. Tell me,' he said, and the glint was visible in his eyes again, 'how *au fait* are you with the Greek financial press?'

The bristles down Vicky's spine stiffened, and deliberately she did not answer.

'As I assumed,' Theo Theakis returned smoothly. 'You will, therefore, be unaware that there is currently a hostile bid in the market for your uncle's company. Without boring you with the ways of stock market manoeuvrings, one way to defend against such an attack is for another company to take a non-hostile financial interest in the target company. This is currently the subject of discussion between your uncle and myself.'

'Are you going to do it?' Vicky asked bluntly.

She could see his eyes veil. 'As I said, it is a subject of current discussion,' he replied.

She looked him straight in the eyes. 'I don't see what on earth this has to do with the insane conversation I've just had with him!' she launched robustly.

Did his face tighten? She didn't know and didn't care.

'Your uncle is a traditionalist,' observed Theo Theakis. 'As such, he considers it appropriate for close financial relationships to be underpinned by close familial ones. A Fournatos-Theakis marriage would be the obvious conclusion.'

Vicky took a deep breath.

'Mr Theakis,' she said, 'this is the most *idiotic* thing I've heard in all my life. Two complete strangers don't just marry because one of them is doing financial deals with the other's uncle! Either there's something more going on than I can spot, or else you're as…unreal…as my uncle! Why on earth don't you just do whatever you intend financially, and get on with it? I've got nothing to do with any of this!'

His expression changed. She could see a plain reaction in it now.

'Unfortunately that is not so.' His voice was crisper, almost abrupt, and the light in his eye had steeled. 'Answer me this question, if you please. How attached are you to your uncle?'

'He's been very kind to me, and apart from my mother he is my only living blood relative,' Vicky replied stiffly. She felt under attack and didn't know why—but she knew she didn't like it.

'Then you have a perfect way to acknowledge that,' came the blunt reply. He leant forward in his seat, and automatically Vicky found herself backing into her chair. 'Aristides Fournatos is a traditionalist, as I said. He is also a proud man. His company is under severe and imminent threat of a hostile acquisition, and his room to manoeuvre against it is highly limited. To put it bluntly, I can save his company for him with a show of confidence and financial strength which will reassure his wavering major institutional shareholders because he is backed by the Theakis Corp. Now, personally, I am more than happy to do that, for a variety of reasons. Hostile bids are seldom healthy for the company acquired, and the would-be acquirer in this instance is known as an asset-stripper, which will dismember the Fournatos group to maximise revenues and award their own directors massive pay rises and stock options. In short, it will pick it apart like a vulture, and I would not want that to happen to any company, let alone Fournatos. However, my reasons for helping to stave off this attack are also personal. My father was close friends with Aristides, and for that reason alone I would not stand by and watch him lose the company to such marauders.'

'But why does that have to involve anything other than a financial deal between you and my uncle?' persisted Vicky.

Cool, dark and quite unreadable eyes rested on her.

'How do you feel about accepting charity, may I ask?' Vicky could feel her hackles rising again, but the deep-timbred voice continued. 'Aristides Fournatos does not wish to accept my financial support for his company without offering something in return.'

'How about offering you some Fournatos shares?' said Vicky.

Theo Theakis's expression remained unreadable.

'Your uncle wishes to offer more.' There was a pause—a distinct one, Vicky felt. Then Theo Theakis spoke again, as if choosing his next words with care. 'As you know, your uncle has no heir. You are his closest relative. This is why he wishes to cement my offer of support to him at this time with marriage to yourself.'

'You're willing to marry me so you can get his company when he dies?' Vicky demanded. If there was scorn in her voice she didn't bother to hide it.

The dark eyes flashed, and the sculpted mouth tightened visibly.

'I'm willing to enter into a marriage with you to make it easier for Aristides to accept my offer to save his company from ruin.' The sardonic look was back in his eyes now. 'Believe me when I say that I would prefer your uncle to accept it unconditionally. However—' he held up an abrupt hand '—your uncle's pride and his self-respect have already taken a battering by allowing his company to be exposed to such danger in the first place. I would not wish to look ungracious at what he is proposing. For him, this is a perfect solution all round. His pride is salved, his self-respect intact, his company is defended, its future is secured. And as for yourself—' the dark eyes glinted again, and Vicky could feel a very strange sensation starting up in her insides '—your future will also be settled in a fashion that your uncle, standing as he feels himself to do in the place of your late father, considers ideal—marriage to a man to whom he can safely entrust you.'

Vicky got to her feet. 'Mr Theakis,' she started heavily, 'you seriously must be living on another planet if you think for a moment that I—'

'Sit down, if you please.'

The instruction was tersely issued. Abruptly, Vicky sat, and then was annoyed with herself that she had.

'Thespinis Fournatos—somewhere between your intemperate reaction, your uncle's very understandable desires and my own unwillingness to stand by helplessly while your uncle's company is taken over we must reach an agreement acceptable to all. Therefore what I propose is this.' His gaze levelled with hers, and he placed his hands flat on the arms of his chair. 'We enter into a formal marriage in the private but mutual understanding that it will be of very limited duration—sufficient merely to see your uncle through this current crisis and satisfy public and social decencies. I believe that when your uncle has his company safe again he will accept the dissolution of our brief marriage and will come to other arrangements for the long-term future of the Fournatos group. If you have the regard for your uncle which you say you have, then you will agree to this proposal.'

Emotions roiled heavily in Vicky's breast. One was resentment at being spoken to as if she were a mix between a simpleton and an ingrate. The other was more complex—and at the same time a lot more simple.

She didn't want to marry Theo Theakis. Not for any reason, period. The very idea was absurd and ludicrous and insane. It was also—

She veered her thoughts away. Pulled her eyes away from him. She didn't like sitting here, this close to him, alone in his huge office. Theo Theakis disturbed her, and she didn't like it. She didn't like it at all.

She forced herself to look at him again. He was still levelling that impassive, unreadable gaze on her, but she could see, deep at the back of his eyes, the glint in it. There was antagonism there, and something else, too, and she liked that least of all.

She jumped to her feet again. This time Theo Theakis did not order her to sit down. She clutched her handbag to her chest and spoke.

'I don't believe there isn't a different way to deal with this,' she said. 'There just has to be!'

And then she walked out.

The problem was, it was one thing to march out of Theo Theakis's executive office in umbrage, but quite another to face her uncle again. It was evident, she realised with a sinking heart, that as far as he was concerned of *course* she would be marrying the man she now knew would be saving his company. That Aristides had kept this information from her only fuelled her sorrow. The awful thing was that, had it not been for her visit to Theo and his brutal explanation of the cruel facts, she would have had no hesitation in telling Aristides, as gently as she could, that she could not possibly entertain the idea of marrying a man who was virtually a stranger. Let alone one who caused such a frisson of hyper-awareness in her every time she set eyes on him.

But because she now knew just how vital it was for her uncle to be able to wrap up Theo Theakis's financial help in a dynastic marriage, she simply could not do it.

Yet how could she *possibly* agree to such a marriage? It was out of the question! Even if it *was* limited to the superficial temporary marriage of convenience that Theo Theakis was advocating.

I can't possibly marry him! It's absurd, ludicrous, ridiculous…

But even though those were the words she deliberately used to describe such a marriage, she could feel her resistance being eroded. The more closely she studied her uncle's face, the more she could see the web of anxiety in it, the fear haunting the back of his eyes. For him, it seemed, everything depended on her accepting this marriage proposal. And as far as her uncle was concerned, Vicky could see, no young woman in her right mind would dream of turning it down! It offered everything—a husband who was not just extremely wealthy but magnetically attractive, who was lusted after by all other females, and held in respect and esteem by all men. What on earth was there to turn down? To her uncle, he was an ideal husband…

It was a clash of worlds, she knew. Her modern world, where you married for love and romance, and his, where you married for family, financial security and social suitability. A clash that could not be resolved—or explained. Every instinct told her that she could not—should not—do what her uncle wanted. And yet her heart squeezed. If she turned down this marriage proposal—even on the terms that Theo Theakis was offering her—the consequences for her uncle would be catastrophic.

I can't do it to him! I can't let him go under! But I can't possibly marry a man I don't know, for any reason whatsoever! But if I don't, then my uncle will be ruined…

Round and round the dilemma went in her head, making dinner that evening a gruelling ordeal. Vicky was horribly aware of the expectant-yet-anxious expression that was constantly in her uncle's eyes, both day and night, and she herself endured a fitful, sleepless night. And so it was with a sense of escape the following morning that she took a telephone call from London.

But her pleasure in hearing Jem's voice swiftly turned to dismay. She had left the running of Freshstart to him while she was in Greece, but before the phone call was over she realised it had been a mistake. Jem was great with kids—he could make emotional contact with the most troubled teenager—but as an organiser and administrator he was, she had to admit, poor.

'I'm really sorry, Vicky, but it seems I didn't get that grant application in on time and the deadline has passed. Now we can't apply again till next year.' Jem's voice was apologetic. 'They were shorthanded with the kids, so I went to help out, and then I was out of time to get the form into the post.'

Vicky suppressed a sigh of irritation. Even with the money her father had left, the charity needed every penny it could raise, and the grant she'd been counting on getting would have gone a long way. Now she had even more on her plate to worry about, despite the unbelievable situation she found herself in here in Greece.

However, soon her attention had to return to that, when, shortly after she'd finished speaking to Jem, there was another phone call for her.

It was Theo Theakis.

'I would like you to join me for lunch,' he informed her with minimal preamble, and told her the name of the restaurant and the time he wanted her to be there. Then he hung up. Vicky stared at the phone resentfully, wishing the man to perdition.

All the same, she presented herself at the designated location at the appointed hour, and slid into her seat as Theo Theakis got to his feet at her approach. Instinctively, she avoided anything but the briefest eye contact with him, and self-consciously ignored the various speculative glances that were obviously coming their way.

Her lunch partner wasted little time in getting to the point.

'I do not wish to harass you, but a decision from you on the matter under consideration is needed without delay,' he began, as soon as the waiter had taken their orders. 'The marauding company has just acquired another tranche of shares. Other shareholders are clearly wavering. Unless a very clear signal is sent to them imminently to say that I am aligning myself with Aristides they will start to sell out in critical numbers. So…' His dark eyes rested on her without expression. 'Once again I must ask you whether you are prepared to accept the recommendation I made to you yesterday.'

She could feel her hands tensing in her lap.

'There *has* to be another way of—' she began tightly.

'There isn't.' Theo Theakis's voice was brusque. 'If there were, I would take it. However, if you are still of the same mind as you were yesterday afternoon—' again Vicky could hear the note of critical condemnation in his voice, and it raised her hackles automatically '—then allow me to mention something that was omitted from our exchange then.'

He paused a moment, and Vicky made herself meet his eyes. They were quite opaque, but there was something in them that was even more disturbing than usual. She wanted to look away, but grimly she held on.

He started to speak again.

'Because of your upbringing in England I appreciate that the concept of a dynastic marriage such as your uncle hopes for is very alien to you. However…' He paused again minutely, as if deciding whether to say what he went on to say. 'There is another aspect of such arrangements which your lack of familiarity with them might require me to make plain to you. It is the matter of the marriage settlement. Although the issue is complicated by the matter of the threat to your uncle's company, nevertheless in simplistic terms the outcome for yourself would be a sum of money set aside—in the form, if you like, of a dowry. No, do not interrupt me, if you please— I appreciate you find the term archaic, but that is irrelevant.'

He broke off while the sommelier approached with the wine he had chosen for lunch, and went through the ritual of tasting it, approving it with a curt assent. Then he continued. There was a slightly different tone to his voice as he spoke now. A smooth note had entered it, and Vicky felt it like a rich, dark emollient over her nerve-endings.

'It must be hard for you,' Theo Theakis said, as he contemplatively took a mouthful of the wine, setting back the glass on the table but never taking his eyes from her. 'Staying with your uncle and appreciating, perhaps for the first time, just how very different your life would have been had your father not been of the philanthropic disposition that he so abundantly was. In the light of that, therefore, and in respect of the sum of money I alluded to, which in the event of a normal marriage would remain with me, I am prepared, since I am proposing a highly limited marriage, to release this sum to you on the dissolution of the marriage.' His veiled gaze rested on her. 'Additionally, I am willing to make you an advance on this sum at the outset of our temporary marriage. The figure I have in mind is this.'

He named a sum of money that made Vicky swallow. It was about three times the amount of the grant that Jem had just failed to apply for.

Her mind raced. With that money they could…

She dragged her thoughts away from all the things that Freshstart could spend that kind of money on, and back to the man sitting opposite her, in his superbly tailored business suit, with his dark, sable hair and his opaque, unreadable eyes that nevertheless seemed to send a frisson through her that went right down to her bones.

'Well?'

She opened her mouth, then closed it again.

'The final sum released to you when our marriage ends would be twice as much again,' he said, into the silence.

Twice as much?

What we could do with such a sum!

She stared, unseeing for a moment, ahead of her, oblivious even of the disturbing figure opposite her. What would her father have done? She could not remember him, but her mother had told her so much about him.

'He gave away his inheritance to those who needed it. He didn't think twice about it.'

Her mother's well-recalled words echoed in her head. She felt her throat tighten. What should she do? If she went ahead with this insane idea she could not only save her uncle's company, but inject into her father's charity a sum of money that would help so many children blighted by poverty and wrecked families…

But I'd have to marry Theo Theakis…

Slowly her eyes refocussed on the man sitting at the far side of the table. The familiar frisson went through her.

If he were just an ordinary person I could do it…

But he wasn't—that was the problem. He was a man like no other she had ever encountered, and to whom she reacted as she had never done in her life before.

It's too dangerous…

The words formed in her mind and etched into her brain cells.

No—it didn't have to be dangerous! In fact—she pressed her lips together determinedly—it was absurd to even think of that word. Absurd because it didn't *matter* that she reacted so strongly to Theo Theakis. The point was that *he* was not reacting to her at all! It was all on her part, and if she just succeeded in keeping a totally tight lid on the way he affected her then she could just go ahead and…

She inhaled sharply. Good God, was she really thinking what she was thinking? Was she really, seriously thinking that she could go ahead with this insane scheme? Surely to God she couldn't be?

Yet she could feel her mouth shaping words, hear them sounding low across the table, coming from somewhere she didn't want to think about.

'How long would we have to stay married?'

* * *

The phone on her desk was ringing, and Vicky heard it from a long, long way away. Sucked down into the past. Painfully, she dragged her mind back to the present—the present in which frustration and bitter anger warred in equal proportions.

'How long would we have to stay married?'

The fateful question she had posed that day over lunch reverberated in her head. It had been the moment that she had mentally acceded to the idea of entering into the kind of marriage that Theo Theakis had outlined to her. She'd known that even at the time.

And he'd started to cheat her from that very moment! Because the kind of marriage he'd outlined had been nothing, *nothing* like it had turned out to be!

He cheated me right from the start—and he went on cheating me right to the end! The brutal, merciless end...

Anger buckled through her again. Oh, Theo Theakis might have paid out upfront all right—the money he'd said was an advance on what he would make over to her when they were finally free to end their marriage—but as for the rest of it...

It's mine! He promised it to me—it's not his to keep!

He's got no business hanging on to it! Just because I...

The insistent ringing of the phone finally broke through her angry reverie. She snatched it up.

'Yes?' she said tersely.

The voice that answered was accented, formal, and studied.

'This is Demetrious Xanthou. I am aide to Theo Theakis. He has instructed me to inform you that he will receive you this evening. If you will be so good as to give me your address, I will arrange a car for 8:00 p.m.'

For ten seconds Vicky went totally still. But the emotions that warred in her were not tranquil. Turmoil seethed in her. Haltingly, hardly able to concentrate, she gave her address. Then, hand shaking only very slightly, she set the phone down.

She stared ahead blindly for a moment. Then her face set again, and a grim, ruthless expression entered her eyes.

She was finally going to get her face-to-face with the man who had rent her limb from limb with his savage words. Well, she wouldn't care about that now—she had one thing only in her sights.

I want that money. It's mine. I want it—and I need it.

And I'm going to make him give it to me—whatever it takes!

It was the only thought she was going to allow herself.

Anything else was much, much too disturbing. Much too dangerous.

Theo Theakis stood by the window of his London apartment, looking out over one of its most historic parks. His face was expressionless, but beneath the impassive exterior one emotion was uppermost.

He rested his eyes on the woman in front of him.

Unlike during her attempt to accost him the day before, she was dressed without the slightest effort to look the part today. It was deliberate; that much was obvious. Yesterday she had been playing the role of Mrs Theo Theakis—even though she no longer had the least right to that name, he thought, with a savage spurt of anger. Tonight she had chosen a different image. Jeans and a chainstore sweat top. Her hair was caught up in a ponytail, and she wore not a scrap of make up.

His lips pressed together. She would not be wearing that outfit for him again—

'Well?'

The voice was curt, demanding. The line of his lips tightened. How dared she stand there, shameless and insolent, and speak to him in such a tone? His eyes darkened.

'You wanted to talk to me. In fact, you were very expres-

sive on the subject.' His voice was clipped, and he didn't bother
to hide the note of sarcasm in it. 'So,' he invited, 'talk.'

He watched her eyes narrow. After all she'd done to him she
still thought she had the right to call the shots. Take umbrage.
Make demands.

Well, she could make them all right—and she could pay the
price, as well.

'I want my money.'

The bald, bare, shameless words fell from her. Theo felt his
tightly controlled anger stab again.

'Your money?' He echoed her words, eyes spearing hers.
'*Your* money? The law takes a different view—as you very well
know. The settlement that Aristides drew up with me is very
clear—the money is mine.'

He could see fury leap in her face, and it gave him grim
amusement. She spat back at him venomously.

'You promised it to me! You told me it would be mine when
the marriage ended! And now you're cheating me of it!'

Anger leapt into his face uncontrolled.

'You *dare* accuse me of cheating?'

Her expression contorted.

'It's my money! And you're keeping it! What the hell else
is it but cheating?' she demanded furiously.

Cold fire poured from him.

'*Christou*, are you really so terminally stupid that you
imagine I would have the *slightest* inclination to let you have
that money? After what you did? You deserved nothing—and
nothing is what you got!' His voice changed, become harsh and
deadly. 'What else does an adulterous wife deserve?'

CHAPTER FOUR

VICKY could feel her face whiten. She was back in the past again, and Theo Theakis was laying into her with his vicious talons, ripping her to shreds with his vituperation. She had tried to defend herself but it had been impossible. He had allowed her no chance—no quarter.

Well, this time she would not even make the attempt. She would not stoop that low.

But it was hard—much, much harder than she had allowed for—to stand here, face to face, with that overpowering presence in front of her, the full force of his self-righteous anger bearing down on her. It was like an intense, overwhelming pressure coming at her, trying to make her buckle and crack. Trying to destroy her.

Her spine steeled. She didn't destroy that easily! She'd survived that first hideous onslaught of his, which had ended their unspeakable farce of a marriage, even though she'd been shaking like a leaf before he'd done with her, desperate only to run, run from his presence as fast as her trembling limbs would carry her.

It might have served its purpose, but that did not mean she could ever forgive or forget that brutal scene, his vicious, self-righteous judgement of her.

So now, gathering a nerve she had to dig deep to find, she slid her hands into her back pockets, shifted the weight of her leg, and looked across at him, her face a mask. Her voice, as she spoke, was cool.

'I'm not here to discuss ancient history, Theo. I'm here to get the money you've been keeping from me. I don't give a toss how our marriage ended, only that it did—and that you owe me.'

As she finished she had the strangest feeling she'd just lit the blue touch paper—but the rocket didn't go up. Instead, something slid across his face, almost as if he were wiping it clear of any expression or emotion. She'd seen him look like that often, usually when he was talking to people but revealing nothing of what was going on inside his head. It had been a common expression when he'd been talking to her, as well.

His tone was smooth suddenly, but with the smoothness of steel. 'We've already established that you have no entitlement to it whatsoever. However...' His eyes rested on her, and there was that same concealed characteristic about them as in his face. 'I may, perhaps, be willing to change my mind. Tell me—' the question came out of the blue '—what do you want the money for?'

Vicky started. Automatically she veiled her expression. No way was she going to tell him that Jem was anything to do with why she wanted the money—the memory of Theo's verbal gouging of her two years ago was too deep for that, and Jem's name would be like a red rag to a bull.

'What business is that of yours?' she countered, still keeping that cool, deliberate voice going.

She could see the anger lick through him at her reply. Theo Theakis was a man who liked getting his own way—she knew that, to her cost. Whatever he wanted, Theo liked to get it.

Even when it was personal.

Especially when it was personal.

And he wasn't fussy about what he was prepared to do to get his own way…

Her mind sheered away. Memory was dangerous, very dangerous. Much safer was Theo being angry with her. His anger might be a vicious onslaught of savage fury, or it might be the cold, contained, implacable power of a very rich man, but both of those were easier to endure than—

No. She cut her mind off again.

Focus! Focus on what you want here—your money. That's all you're here for. Nothing else! Nothing else at all.

But if that were true, why—dear God—did her eyes keep wanting to smooth over that tall, lean body standing so short a distance away from her? To rest on that planed, ludicrously compelling face and just gaze and gaze, like a hungry animal long deprived of food…?

He was replying to her, and she forced herself to listen.

'It's a substantial amount of money. You are not used to being in possession of such sums. Therefore you may be the target of unscrupulous operators who wish to part you from it.' His voice was smooth, the lick of anger gone completely now from the visible surface.

But Vicky remained wary—she knew she had every reason to be.

'I'm putting it in the bank, that's all. I want to spend some of it on a house, the rest stays in the bank.'

It was an evasive answer, and she knew it. True in some sense, but implying, falsely, that she wanted to buy a house, not do one up, and that there would be a lot left over—when there would probably be none at all. But she didn't owe Theo Theakis the truth. She didn't owe him anything.

She held his gaze, resolutely keeping hers steady.

'Very prudent,' he murmured, and again Vicky got the feeling that there were currents running deep beneath that smooth surface.

But what did she care about those, either? She just cared about getting her money. That was all.

'Very well—I'll release the money.'

The words fell into the space between them—and that was much, much more than the few metres that separated them. For a second she stood still, not believing she could have heard right. Then her eyes lit—she could not stop them.

'But there will, of course, need to be conditions.'

His voice was smooth still. So smooth.

The light in her eyes flashed into anger.

'You have absolutely *no* right to—'

His hand came up abruptly. 'What I have,' he enunciated, 'is something you want, and if you want it then you accept my conditions.'

She was the insubordinate minion again. Her chin came up in defiance.

'And they are?' she demanded, eyebrows rising with the same cool deliberation she'd used before.

His eyes rested on her a moment. She could not read them—could not read the smooth surface of his expression. But suddenly, quite suddenly, out of nowhere, the barest fraction before he spoke, acid pooled in her stomach.

'They're very simple,' he said. 'You'll return to Greece with me, and to my bed.'

The acid leached from Vicky's stomach and into her veins, draining down into every limb.

'You *cannot* mean that,' she breathed. It seemed to take all the breath she had left in her lungs to do so. Her eyes had widened like a rabbit's, seeing a predator step in front of it.

Something flickered in the back of his eyes, and she felt her lungs crush yet more.

'It's exactly what I mean. If you want the money, you'll comply.' His voice was unperturbed.

'It's *outrageous*!'

'So is adultery.' His voice was cold, as cold as steel.

'I won't do it.' Her teeth were gritted, so tight it hurt.

He shrugged, the material of his jacket moving over broad shoulders.

'Then there's nothing more to be said, is there? So you'd better go, hadn't you? But if you do—' his voice hardened '—don't trouble to get in touch again. You decide now—right now—what you intend to do.'

She stood transfixed, staring at him horror. And from behind the horror came memories, marching forward, one after another, like the frames of a movie, surging forward in vivid, punishing colour…memories she never, ever allowed herself…

I can't do it! Dear God, I can't!

'Well?'

She could feel her stomach churning with acid.

'No! God Almighty, of *course* I won't do it! You must be insane to think I would!'

'Very well. If that's your decision.' He started to move towards the door.

She spun round. 'I want my money!' Her voice was all but a shriek of anger and frustration—and horror.

'Then comply with my conditions.' His voice was cool, impersonal. He didn't even look round, simply walked out into the hall and made to open the door of his apartment.

She strode after him, the acid still churning in her stomach.

'*Why*? Why the hell do you even want to…to…?'

She couldn't say it—it was impossible. As impossible as believing he'd actually said that to her!

He turned. For a moment he was still, very still. She stood, her insides churning. Then suddenly, before she had a chance to realise his intent, he reached out a hand to her.

Long fingers slid around her jaw, grazing into her hair. His eyes looked down at her. Their expression jellied her stomach.

With leisurely insolence his thumb grazed along her lower lip. The touch shot weakness through her body.

'I like to finish what I start,' he said.

His thumb smoothed again. She couldn't move. She was transfixed, her heart slugging in her chest. Then he smiled. The smile of a predator. He dropped his hand away.

'I'm flying to Athens tomorrow at noon in my private place. You have till then to make up your mind what you're going to do.'

He pulled the door open and waited, expectantly, for her to go.

On shaking legs she left.

London flowed around her like an unseen river as she walked blindly along its darkened streets. At some point she must have walked down into the Underground system and taken a train, changed to a different line, kept going, emerged, and walked back to her tiny studio flat. When she got indoors she went into the kitchen, and with the same disconnected brain started to make herself a cup of tea. Then, on sudden desperate impulse, she poured herself a glass of white wine, took a large gulp as she headed to the living area, and collapsed on the sofa.

She stared blankly ahead. She could feel her heart thumping in her chest.

I've got to think about this. I can't not think about it. I don't want to think about it. I don't want to do anything other than pretend that whole encounter tonight just didn't happen. Deny it completely. Wash it from my brain, my memory, my consciousness.

But I can't. I can't do that because I know, though I desperately don't want to. I know I've got to make a decision.

She took a second gulp of the alcohol. Another voice seemed to shoot through her brain.

What the hell do you mean, you've got to make a decision? There isn't any decision to be made! You can't possibly, possibly think otherwise! What he said is unthinkable—it's disgusting and outrageous, and he can damn well go to hell for even saying it to you!

She stared ahead still. Her heart seemed to be thumping more heavily, and there was a sick feeling inside her, like nerve-ends pinching in her guts.

But he said it was the only way I can get my money...

The other voice slammed back. *Well, you'll just have to do without it, then!*

She swallowed heavily. Do without it. But they couldn't. That was the problem. Without the money that she'd promised Jem there was no way the house could be ready for the summer—which meant they'd have to wait another season before being able to take in any kids, if ever. The whole scheme depended on her getting the money.

We need that money! We've just got to have it!

Anger spurted through her again. Theo had no *right* to that money! It didn't matter what the damn law said, the money was for *her*, at the end of their stupid, insane marriage, and him keeping it was sheer bloody vindictiveness! Petty revenge, that was all!

She took another vicious gulp of wine. It was coursing through her system, making her feel angry and aggressive.

It was a marriage of convenience. That was the whole point! Something just to keep Aristides happy, to make him able to accept Theo Theakis's help without losing face. That's all I went along with it for! And that's what Theo said, too! A temporary marriage of convenience, for my uncle's sake.

Indignation burned along her veins.

It had been a deliberate, business-based marriage of convenience, and therefore obviously, *obviously*, the issue of fidelity was irrelevant! How could anyone think otherwise?

Her face darkened. But Theo Theakis had. The all-time original dinosaur—with vicious talons and an even more vicious tongue, that had verbally ripped her to bloodied shreds before he'd done with her!

Angrily she answered him in her head—the way she had that terrible day when he'd confronted her.

It was a marriage of convenience, Theo! Not a real one! An empty façade, meaning nothing—nothing at all! And you damn well should have treated it as such, instead of…instead of—

Her mind cut out. No. No, no and *no*. She wasn't to think of that—never. Ever. Forbidden. Locked door. Never to be opened.

Except that tonight, to her face, Theo had opened that door and made her look inside.

Her face drained of expression. She knew what Theo wanted. His taunting, insolent words formed in her brain— *'I like to finish what I started.'* But that wasn't why he'd made that outrageous condition tonight. It had nothing to do with it. He wanted something quite different.

Revenge.

And he knew exactly, *exactly*, how to get it.

A shudder went through her.

Adultery—that had been the crime that Theo had thrown so viciously in her face. So unjustly.

She could have defended herself in terms that even he would have had to accept—but if she had…

No, that had been impossible! It had been impossible then, and it was impossible now.

And for the same reason.

Her fingers clenched around the wineglass, threatening to break the stem. She must not, *must not*, let her mind go in that direction. It wasn't just dangerous—it was suicidal…

Desperately she pulled her mind away from the precipice it tottered on. Adultery was not the only crime she had committed in Theo's eyes. There was another, far, far worse, and he wanted revenge for that, too.

And he would get it, she knew, with a terrible chilling in her guts. The revenge that he would exact from her would be an exercise in humiliation.

Her humiliation.

And Theo would extract every last gram from her until he was satisfied—satisfied that her crime against him had been paid for.

I can't go through with it! I can't! It's impossible! Impossible!

Anguish filled her, and she could feel herself start to shake.

I can't face the humiliation—I can't face Theo taking that revenge on me! I can't!

Abruptly she got to her feet, and went and refilled her wineglass. She took another large slug from it, and stared blindly around her small studio flat. It was a world away, a universe away, from the life she'd led in Athens as Mrs Theo Theakis.

I can't possibly go back there!

How could she ever go back there? She could never do it to her uncle, for a start. Since leaving Greece so precipitately she had not seen Aristides. She had written him a stiff, painful letter, simply saying that, regrettably, her marriage to Theo Theakis had 'broken down irretrievably' and left it at that. She had not received a reply or any communication from her uncle since. She knew why. Theo had told him why he had taken an axe to their marriage.

Her face darkened. Why the hell had Theo gone and done that? There had been no need—no need whatsoever! What he had accused her of had never been made public, and however much speculation there might have been in the gossiping circles of Athenian society it had remained merely that—gossip.

Theo could just have told her uncle that their marriage had broken down, without having to spell out why. After all, that was precisely what they had been going to do anyway, by prearrangement. She had merely precipitated their divorce, nothing more…

Merely…

The word mocked her. There had been nothing 'merely' about it.

Not for her and not, she knew—dear God, she knew!—for Theo, either.

And now he wanted his revenge for it.

Why had he waited this long?

The answer followed hard on the question. *Because you've handed him the possibility on a plate by demanding your money! He's got you over a barrel, and if you want the money you'll have to do what he wants…*

But she couldn't. It was as simple as that.

She would never, ever subject herself to the humiliation he had planned for her. Because that was what it would be, she knew—oh, how she knew! A calculated, assiduous, deliberate humiliation of her…

Her eyes narrowed suddenly. Her body stilled.

Why? Why does it have to be? That was what Theo would want—but why did she have to comply?

Why didn't she simply…simply refuse to play along?

Or rather…

Her narrowed eyes hardened, and she took another belligerent slug of wine.

Theo wanted revenge—and his revenge would be in her humiliation at his hands.

A tight, grim smile twisted her lips. Revenge? Well, revenge was a two-way street. A double-edged sword. Theo intended to sweep one edge of the sword down on her—but she could use the other side of the blade for her own ends.

Not revenge. Something far, far more important to her.

She drained her wineglass. The alcohol was swimming in

her veins, but she welcomed it. Dutch courage? Possibly—but it was steeling her, giving her the resolve she needed. Needed to get through what lay ahead of her. But if she did it, if she went through with the outrage that Theo was plotting to perpetrate on her, then when it was over she would emerge with something she had never possessed before.

And it had nothing, absolutely nothing, to do with the money she wanted.

Her chin lifted.

I can do this. I can do it. And when I've done it I'm going to walk off with the money that's mine, and Theo Theakis can go to hell!

She set her empty glass down in the sink.

I can do it, she said again to herself. *I can.*

I must.

Because if she did—if she succeeded… Emotion ran through her like a river of lightning in her veins. If she succeeded, then at last…at *last*…she could finally be free of the man she had married. Free in every sense of the word.

*I can do it…*she repeated. *I can…*

It was a mantra she had to keep repeating to herself over the following hours. Otherwise she knew she would never have been able to travel the distance to the aerodrome where Theo Theakis's chartered jet would be waiting to whisk him home at luxurious speed and convenience. She'd deliberately underdressed, wearing jeans and a cheap sweater, with a backpack hoisted on her shoulders. Her hair was in a loose plait and she wore no make-up. Despite the chilly, cloudy weather she wore a pair of sunglasses—but it wasn't the sun they were protecting her from. She had no intention of risking eye contact with Theo.

But even just setting eyes on him again, shielded as she was by her dark glasses, was an ordeal. For one awful moment, as she saw his tall figure swing round towards her, it was all she could do to stop herself turning tail and running as far and as fast as she could.

There was nothing in his eyes as they flicked over her. Neither satisfaction that she'd given in to his despicable terms nor disdain at her scruffy appearance. He simply said something briefly in Greek to the young man standing rather upright and nervously attentive at his side, who promptly came up to her.

'I am Demetrious Xanthou—Mr Theakis's aide. Please let me know if there is anything you would like for the flight.'

He was new to Vicky. She didn't remember him from before. His manner was impeccably polite, but the expression on his face was studiedly incurious. The word 'discretion' all but shrieked from him.

'I'm fine, thanks,' she answered. She tried to make her voice offhand, as if it were nothing that Theo Theakis's ex-wife was flying off to Greece with him two days after throwing her handbag at him in a fit of temper.

It certainly seemed nothing to Demetrious Xanthou, and her face tightened, little more to his employer.

Well, she thought grimly, if Theo wanted to treat her like the invisible woman she should be glad of it! She was only too happy to treat *him* as the invisible man.

Except that it was very difficult to do that. As they boarded the plane, Theo letting her board first with a gesture that was light years away from true consideration but merely social habit, she was horribly conscious of him following her, too close behind. The interior of the jet, with its huge leather seats and mahogany tables—light years away from flying economy class—caught at her suddenly. Memory jabbed into her, sharp and intrusive.

Private jets, squillion-pound yachts, supercars and designer wardrobes—a lifestyle that was the stuff of dreams for so many.

But not for her. For her it had turned into a nightmare.

Abruptly she dropped herself down in the seat she hoped would be furthest away from Theo, and dumped her backpack at her feet. She refused both offers of help to take it from her or to stow it, and busied herself pulling out a paperback from a side pocket, clipping her seat belt across her in a businesslike fashion, and settling down to read. Determinedly, she kept her nose in the book, pausing only to look out of the porthole window for takeoff, which never failed to bring a rush of adrenaline to her, until the jet had reached its cruising altitude. Across the wide aisle she could see that Theo had settled himself down and was talking incisively in Greek to Demetrious, who had a sheaf of papers laid out on the table between them.

The mellifluous tones of the language of her father tugged at her. Since her marriage had ended she'd avoided anything Greek like the plague. Even though she had never managed to learn the language beyond anything other than hesitant reading and simple conversation, hearing Theo give instructions to his aide brought the words teasing back into her mind. And words that were more than business terms…

She felt her stomach plunge, her skin contract over her flesh. All her Dutch courage of the night before had vanished completely. All her vain resolve to turn this outrageous situation to her own advantage was gone—completely gone! All that remained was panic—blind, blind, panic. She was sitting on Theo's plane, being flown back to Greece.

He's going to have sex with me, and I've consented! My very presence on this plane is my consent!

She must have been mad! She would have to run—run the moment the plane landed. Use her credit card to buy a return flight and get out the moment she could!

But if she did she would never get her money.

Jem would never get her money. Pycott Grange wouldn't be able to open that summer. Children who needed it desperately would have to do without. And she—she would not achieve what last night had seemed finally within her grasp…

Her ultimate freedom from the power that Theo Theakis wielded over her. The power she dreaded more than anything else in the world…

You've got to do it. You've got to—it's the only way.

Just don't think about it—don't think about it till you have to.

Hurriedly, she scrabbled about in the rucksack for her music and stuck headphones in her ears, flicking on the soothing counterpointed intricacies of Bach, instantly silencing the rest of the world around her. Doggedly she forced herself to keep reading. When, a little later, the smiling stewardess came to ask her what she would like by way of refreshments, she asked for coffee, refusing the champagne that was proffered. The very thought of alcohol now was stomach churning. So was food. Acid was running in her stomach, and she felt sick.

But she mustn't, *mustn't* let it show! To let Theo see her nerves would be to pander to his vicious need for revenge, and she would not, *would not* give him that satisfaction.

At least he was not in her line of sight, and nor could she hear his deep, dark voice any more, and for that she could be grateful. When her coffee arrived she lifted the cup, taking little sips, staring out of the window over the fleecy cloudscape, willing herself to be calm as the *Brandenburg Concertos* wove their compelling rhythm through her head. The morning had been such a rush she'd had no time to do anything other than surface, groggily, after a restless, tormented night of unpeaceful intermittent sleep and tearing emotion, then throw the essentials into her backpack.

As for Jem—she'd changed her mind half a dozen times about whether to phone him and tell him she was on the trail of the money. Half of her wanted to reassure him, but half was terrified he'd start asking her questions about how she'd finally managed to change Theo's mind…

Jem must never know. Never. He would be outraged, and rightly so. No, she mustn't think about Jem. She must keep him ignorant for his own sake, to protect him. Just as she'd kept him ignorant about how brutal Theo had been when he had ended their marriage so precipitately. She'd done so partly to protect Jem, but also because he'd have been bound to storm off and confront Theo on her behalf, and then Theo would know…

No—she cut off her thoughts abruptly. Jem now, like then, had to be kept out of this. This was between her and Theo. That was all. She and Jem went back a long, long way, and he was vitally important to her—but she didn't want him dragged back into the ungodly mess that had been the ending of her farcical marriage.

I'll do what I have to do—achieve what I aim to achieve. Then I'll come home again, to Jem, hand him the money, and never say a word of what I had to do to get it.

What I'm going to have to do…

As she sat, tense as a board, sipping hot coffee, the full enormity of what she was doing hit her like slugs to her chin. Disbelief drenched through her, and a sense of dissociation from reality that she had been clinging to for dear life.

I can do this—I can.

I must.

The mantra went round her head, carried by Bach, stopping her thinking of anything else. Anything at all.

And especially, above all, what 'this' would actually mean…

She could feel her eyes flickering and managed to replace the coffee cup on the table in front of her, her head starting to loll. Her restless, tormented night was catching up with her.

The dream she slipped into was vivid. Instant.

She was on the island. That magical, maquis-clad island,

where the azure bowl of the sky cupped land lapped by a cobalt sea, enclosing it in a private, secret world, a world where the outside world ceased to exist, where everything—everyone—was reduced to the elements of which they were made. Sky and stone, sand and sea, air and water, light and dark. Flesh and blood.

And heat. Heat beating up through the rocks, burning down from the blazing sun, heat running in her veins like a fire. A fire she could not quench, a heat she could not cool, heat in her skin, her veins, her nerves, her flesh…flushing through her, pulse, after pulse, after pulse…

She woke—eyes wide, staring. Heart pounding. Terrified.

Words screamed through her.

I can't do this! I can't! I can't! I can't!

Her hands clenched over the arms of her seat.

The plane flew on.

Theo listened as Demetrious brought him up to date on a dozen different items on his always crowded agenda. But his mind was elsewhere.

So she had come. He had half wondered if she would. It could have gone either way, he knew—her self-righteous fury was quite capable of cutting off her own nose to spite her face. His face tightened. It was that, above all, that enraged him— her self-righteousness! Her self-righteous fury at being denied what she dared, *dared* to consider her entitlement to her uncle's money! The uncle she had insulted and shamed, who even now still felt the burden of what she had done.

As for himself—the lines around his mouth incised more deeply—did she really think she could do what she had done and then expect him to meekly hand over the money? His eyes flickered to where he could just see the edge of her body, almost invisible to him. He felt again that stab of raw black anger go through him. Then another emotion countered it.

Should he have made her this offer, given her the chance to get the money she craved? Shouldn't he just have continued to stonewall her, ignore her very existence, as he had done since he had thrown her out, raining down on her the censure she so richly deserved?

With his head he knew that that was indeed what he should have done—every gram of sense in him told him so.

But sense was not uppermost in his mind now. He knew that, deplored it, and yet even so knew he was going to pursue this— knew he was going to carry out what he had every intention of doing. What he had promised her last night when he'd felt again the touch of her flesh against his.

He had unfinished business with her.

And only when he had finished it—finished with her— would he finally throw her from his life permanently.

CHAPTER FIVE

As the plane made its final descent, Vicky felt her stomach acid go into overdrive again. Not just because she was that much closer in time to the ordeal ahead of her. Nor just because of the nightmare memories that were ready to spring like banshees into her brain, with every familiar sight of Greece around her. But because something else had dawned on her—something that would make the ordeal ahead even worse. Where, exactly, was Theo planning on taking her—and did he intend her to be seen with him in public? On show at his side…?

Dear God, surely he can't be planning to do that?

She swallowed. That had turned out to be the worst aspect of her brief, ill-fated marriage. It was ironic, really. It had been, after all, purely for show that she had gone along with the insane idea of marrying him in the first place! To show the world that Aristide Fournatos was not going cap in hand to Theo Theakis to save his company, but was merely doing something that every Greek family could approve of: forging a link for the mutual benefit of both commercial dynasties, between his niece and a suitable—oh, so highly suitable—husband. Saving his company was almost incidental.

And so being on show had been an essential part and purpose of their marriage. Vicky had thought she could cope with it—

after all, a marriage for external show only was all she had signed up for.

But it had proved far, far more difficult than she had ever imagined.

And then—impossible…

Quite, quite impossible…

She tensed in recollection as the memories started to march across her brain.

As Aristides Fournatos's niece she had been of interest to her uncle's circle of friends and acquaintances, accepted by them despite her Englishness, because of Aristides. But as the wife of Theo Theakis she'd become an object not of interest, but of almost virulent curiosity.

Especially from women, and in particular—the gleeful words of her uncle that every woman in Athens would envy her had not been an exaggeration—women to whom her husband was an object of their sexual interest.

There were so many of them. Women like the one who had commandeered him the evening she had first been introduced to him at her uncle's dinner party, women who had quite obviously either had an affair with him or wanted one. Or wanted another one. Athens, it seemed, was awash with women who found the man she had married magnetically attractive, and who all shared something in common—envy of her, or resentment, or both. Vicky had soon realised that she had committed a social solecism of the highest order—she had walked off with the prize matrimonial catch in Greek society.

Without deserving it.

Crime enough—except for something even worse.

Without appreciating it…

Her gaze hardened.

Vicky knew, as the jet made its descent, that she had spectacularly failed to appreciate the enviable good fortune of having Theo Theakis for a husband. The needling and barbed comments she had received from other women had been proof enough of that. Comments openly directed at her by women congratulating her on her great good fortune in capturing such a prize, as well as more malicious observations from women who had, with sweetly smiling insincerity, expressed the hope that Theo Theakis would manage to be as interested in her as a bride as he evidently was in her uncle's company. Her studiedly blank reaction in the face of all this antagonism had seemed to irritate them even more. The provocation had got worse, making her dread those social occasions when she'd had to be on show with Theo, until finally, to her relief, she had been castigated as a cold-blooded Englishwoman, dull and passionless, and dismissed from their further attention.

But it hadn't just been the scores of women for whom Theo Theakis was an object of desire who had regarded her marriage to Theo as a big mistake

Her eyes darkened balefully and her hands clamped in her lap involuntarily.

She knew to the exact moment when she had realised, with a terrifying hollowing of her stomach, just how big a mistake she had made when she had finally agreed to marry Theo.

Talk about being lulled into a false sense of security...

She had always, right from the start, been a reluctant bride. Quite apart from anything else, the terms of her marriage had meant deceiving her mother and stepfather. It had appalled her when she'd realised that Aristides had been planning to invite them to Athens for the wedding, and she'd had to urgently cite her parents' inability to take leave in the middle of the school term to stop him doing so. She had also lied to him, saying that she had told them about her marriage. Of course she had not! If her mother had got the slightest whiff that her daughter was marrying a man she scarcely knew, for the reasons she was doing so, she would have been on the first flight to Athens to stop her!

Telling Jem had been imperative, of course—if for no other reason than he'd wanted to know when she was going to take over at Freshstart again. It had been incredibly awkward telling him, and even though she had assured him fervently that it was of *course* a marriage in name only, she knew he'd been dismayed by her decision to go ahead with it. Even the knowledge that as soon as it was decent she would end the marriage and return to the UK with a handsome donation to her father's charity had not made him warm to it. Nor had he relished having to run Freshstart in her absence, even though she'd promised him she would only be, after all, at the end of a phone if he needed her. But it had been yet another complication, and the more she'd got sucked into the whole business of marrying Theo Theakis, for however short a duration, the more reluctant she'd become—and the more inextricable her commitment had become, as well.

Only the visible relief in her uncle's eyes had kept her going. That, and one other thing. Since making the fateful decision she had spent minimal time with Theo, during which he had treated her with an impersonal formality that had managed to get her through the ordeal not just of the brief betrothal period but the wedding, as well. Despite the wedding being nothing more than a business arrangement it had been conducted with jaw-dropping extravagance. A lavish civil ceremony—to her uncle's disappointment—had been followed by a huge reception, during which she'd stood at Theo's side, stiff and disbelieving at what she had just done.

It hadn't been until they'd arrived at their honeymoon destination that the reality had hit her with the force of a sledge-hammer. There had been something about being ushered into the honeymoon suite of a five-star hotel with the doors closing on her and Theo that had brought home to her the fact that in the eyes of the world he was her husband.

There was, she had realised, staring in horror, only one bedroom—and only one bed.

She had turned in the doorway. Theo had been behind her.

'What is it?' he asked, seeing her aghast expression. His enquiry was brisk.

'There's only one bed,' she said.

His eyes glanced past her shoulder. Then they went to her face. For one brief moment something flickered in his eyes. Then it was gone. He gave a shrug.

'It's the honeymoon suite. What did you expect?'

She took a step backwards. Already the bellhop had deposited their suitcases in the bedroom. One by each of the vast wardrobes. At the touch of a bell, the maid service would arrive to unpack them, lay out their nightclothes on the bed…

Did he wear any?

The thought formed in Vicky's mind, and the moment it was there she could not undo it. Worse, an instant image accompanied it—Theo's tall, lean frame, stripped of its five-thousand-euro suit…stripped right down to the hard, muscled flesh beneath…

She gulped. No! Dear God, that was no way to begin this totally fake marriage! There was only one way to get through this to the other side—the way Theo had been behaving. As if they were nothing more than passing strangers, temporarily sharing accommodation.

But that's just what we are. Passing strangers…

For the briefest moment emotion shafted through her. For an even briefer moment she recognised it for what it was—and was horror-struck. No—she could not *possibly* be feeling regret that they were nothing more than passing strangers.

She steeled herself mercilessly. Oh, sure, Theo Theakis was compellingly masculine—but what the hell had that to do with the current situation? The whole point of this set-up was not to take any notice of her awareness of him, to completely and resolutely ignore it. Because what would be the point of doing otherwise? Theo Theakis had entered into a temporary, unreal marriage to save her uncle's company. And nothing... *nothing*...else came into the question!

And it wasn't just her who thought so. Even as Theo made his remark he glanced behind him, his gaze picking out the long three-seater sofa in the sitting room behind them.

'I'll sleep on that,' he told her.

That idiotic emotion fleeted through her again as she registered what he intended, and again Vicky tossed it aside and stamped on it. Hard. Very hard.

'Thank you,' she said stiffly.

'Not at all,' said Theo. His voice was formal. There was an inflexion in it she did not pick up.

Their sleeping arrangements set the tone for the rest of the honeymoon—which Theo passed in meetings with various government trade officials and other businessmen, and Vicky in sightseeing tours—and continued thereafter when they returned to Athens, to take up residence in the huge Theakis mansion in an exclusive district of the city. There, they hardly ever saw each other, and Vicky was grateful. The house was so large it was easy to keep out of his way, though she was always relieved when he went off on business to other parts of Europe or, better still, farther afield to America.

It was quite difficult enough coping with the bizarre situation she was in without him being around to add to the strain. Being Mrs Theo Theakis was just that much easier when he wasn't around.

Not that it solved her other problem—boredom. The main occupation of the social circle she found herself in seemed to be spending money and socialising with each other, neither of which Vicky took pleasure in. Shopping seemed mindlessly extravagant, and because of the prurient envy and resentment that she so often received from other women, socialising was out of the question. She would have happily spent more time with her uncle, had it not been clear that right now, as was understandable, his prime concern was his business—seeing off the corporate raider now that he had accepted the financial support of Theakis Corp. Besides which, she was also worried she might let slip just how much of a contrived sham her marriage was.

To pass the time she explored Athens, and all the cornucopia of ancient sites in this region of Greece. She also, inspired by discovering the heritage of her father, started to learn Greek, struggling with the difficulty of the alien script to get to the language it embodied, as well as assiduously studying Greek history, art and philosophy. Then there were concerts, opera and the ballet to divert her, and she became a regular at the theatre. Back at the Theakis mansion she also spent a good two hours a day in the pool, swimming lengths, as well as making the most of the fully equipped gym.

But that, as it turned out, was the easy bit of her marriage. Much, much worse was the time—far too much of it!—when Theo was back in Athens and they had to take part in what seemed to her a never-ending round of social activities. She didn't want to, but it was, she conceded, all part of the show that was the purpose of their marriage in the first place.

But being part of a 'couple' with Theo was a highly uncomfortable process. She felt eyes on her, curious and critical, only adding to her feelings of acute self-consciousness in the role she was being required to play. It was the reason, she knew, that she was so particularly stiff in her manners, and the reason why, too, though she was forced to buy ridiculously expensive clothes for such occasions, she always chose styles that were above all discreetly understated—outfits that did not emphasise or overly reveal her figure, or make her conspicuous. They might draw disdainful looks from the chicly sophisticated women from whom Theo Theakis selected his sexual partners, but what did she care?

Her concern was simply to get through the ordeal of being Mrs Theo Theakis. Constantly at her husband's side, conscious all the time—punishingly so—of his tall, commanding presence beside her, was making it impossible, quite impossible, for her ever to relax.

The hardest occasions, she came to realise, were those when she had to play the role of Mrs Theo Theakis in his house, entertaining others. It seemed to exacerbate her pointless, enervating awareness of him, to put her in an oh-so-visible position where she was indelibly linked to him. Bride of a man that other women wanted and resented her for having.

Help yourselves! she wanted to shout at them.

And especially one of them.

She'd glided up to Theo at one of the social events Vicky had attended with him on their return from their fake honeymoon, and Vicky had recognised her instantly. She was the spectacularly svelte woman who had had been at her uncle's dinner party the evening she had been introduced to Theo, who had been all over him, ignoring Vicky completely.

She ignored her now, too.

'Theo!' Her voice was a rich purr, and she spoke Greek, effectively cutting out Vicky while she used a low, intimate voice to the man at her side. She stood too close to him, in his body space, and the contrast between her closeness and the stiff distance that Vicky habitually kept from Theo was marked. So, too, Vicky registered, with a sudden tension in her muscles, was the difference in the smile that Theo bestowed on the woman.

It was a smile of familiarity—sensuality.

He's never smiled at me like that...

The words formed in her head before she could stop them. Immediately she dismissed them. Of course Theo had never smiled at her like that—it was a smile for a lover to give a woman whose pleasures he had enjoyed.

Not for a woman he'd married in a token arrangement for the sole purpose of saving her uncle's beleaguered company. A woman who meant absolutely nothing else to him…

Forcibly, she stiffened her spine. What on earth was she thinking of? Let him have as many lovers as he wanted. It was nothing to do with her.

And this woman now wasn't anything to do with her, either.

To prove it, she held out her hand.

'Hello—we haven't met yet, have we? I'm sure I would have remembered you,' she said sweetly.

The woman's sloe-like eyes flickered to her. Vicky's voice had been bland, deliberately sticking to English, but she could see the other woman register the subtle insult. Theo's lover—past or present—was not a woman that other women forgot having seen before.

'Christina Poussos,' she returned dismissively. 'An old friend of your…husband.' She hesitated pointedly before giving the descriptor of the man she was too close to.

Vicky's smile was even sweeter.

'Oh, no,' she murmured in a saccharine voice. 'Not that old, surely?'

Her gaze upon the other woman's immaculately made up, thirty-something face was limpid.

At her side, she could hear Theo clear his throat suddenly. She almost frowned. That couldn't possibly have been a smothered laugh, could it?

Then he was intervening, his voice smooth and emollient.

'Christina—Victoria, as I'm sure you know, is Aristides Fournatos's niece.'

The other woman smiled. It was her turn for a shot now, and she took aim pointedly.

'Of course—and I'm sure you will both allow me to congratulate you on an excellent match. Fournatos and Theakis—a formidable commercial combination. And now, my dear Theo,' she went on, having relegated her lover's marriage to nothing more than a corporate merger, 'you must tell me when you will be free for lunch. I need your business acumen in selecting the best investment of my divorce settlement.' She reverted to Greek, once more cutting out Vicky.

Vicky could feel her muscles tense again. If the woman was talking investments in that slinky voice she'd eat her non-existent hat! She stood there, a fixed, doggedly polite smile on her face, sipping at her glass of wine, until with a final throaty laugh Christina Poussos reached up, brushed her mouth against Theo's, and glided off again.

'Until Friday, then, Theo darling,' she murmured, in a Parthian shot that found its mark dead on Vicky, whose fingers suddenly tightened around the stem of her wineglass.

Forcibly she made herself relax them. She didn't care *squat* what Theo got up to with Christina Poussos. Or anyone else.

Deliberately she raised her wineglass and took a larger mouthful than usual.

I don't care. I don't care squat.

Not even microsquat...

And why should she? She hadn't even *wanted* to marry Theo Theakis, so of course she didn't give squat about him carrying on with any women. She just didn't particularly want to know about it, that was all.

Brightly, she turned to Theo, fuelled by the wine inside her.

'Sorry about making that bitchy remark about her age. A bit of a low shot. I do hope I didn't hurt her feelings.'

Theo's dark gaze swept over her before answering. She pinned the bright look to her face with sustained effort.

'I'd say she got her own back quite easily, wouldn't you?' One eyebrow quirked sardonically.

Vicky widened her eyes. 'What, talking about the commercial advantages of a Fournatos-Theakis marriage? What's bitchy about that? It's only the truth.' Her tone was dismissive. 'So long as she doesn't blab to my uncle that it's a totally fake, totally temporary marriage. Speaking of my uncle—isn't that him over there?' She craned her neck slightly, seeing past the people around her. 'Yes, it's definitely him. I'll go over and· say hello. I can't stick here by your side like I'm on a string all evening.'

She made to move, but a light touch on her arm stayed her. Theo's long fingers loosely circled her wrist. She felt a current of electricity go through her that dismayed her, and she froze.

'Why not?' Theo's voice was easy, but she could discern something underneath it—some note that made her muscles tense yet again. 'We are newlyweds, after all.'

She gave a pointed shrug. 'Oh, if you think the show must go on, so be it. Shall we go arm in arm?' she said, with deliberately heavy, terse jocularity.

'Why not?' said Theo again, with smooth assent this time, and now there was a blandness in his voice that somehow managed to grate at her. He tucked her arm into his and drew her forwards towards her uncle. Stiff as a board, Vicky went with him.

The moment she could, she disengaged.

She knew it was only for show, but it didn't make it any easier. Keeping her distance from Theo Theakis was the only way to get through this ordeal.

Her mood was bleak. What the hell had she gone and let herself in for? She wanted to go home—to London, to Jem, to Freshstart, and her safe, familiar world.

A long, long way from Theo Theakis and her ridiculous fake marriage that meant nothing, nothing at all to either of them.

And let's keep it that way! she thought vehemently.

It was far, far too disturbing to think of anything else.

But at least, to her relief, she only had to play the part of Mrs Theo Theakis in public. In private, audience gone, she could finally go off duty and let the tension racking her slacken off. And Theo could, too. He could drop all the pretence he had to put on of being the attentive husband and do nothing more than treat her with indifferent civility, his expression completely neutral. When he spoke to her she might have been anyone—anyone at all—fifteen or fifty, male or female. She was glad of it, and told herself so. It was totally abundantly obvious that Theo Theakis was as indifferent to her as she could possibly want. Off duty, she could revert to the truth of what she and Theo were to each other. Passing strangers who'd united to help her uncle in the only way he would accept help.

Nothing more at all.

Until that fatal evening. That fatal moment.

When she realised that she was facing a danger she had never, ever dreamt she would have to face.

It came right at the end of a large, gruelling dinner party. It had not been an easy evening—such evenings never were—but she had done her best, wearing a carefully selected designer gown and appropriate jewellery, her hair styled, her face perfect, every inch the immaculate hostess, smiling and conversing and being very grateful that the expert Theakis staff kept everything running like clockwork. It had gone on and on, and her face muscles were aching as much as her feet in their elegant narrow shoes. But finally it was over, and the last of the guests took their leave. She stood at the foot of the stairs that swept grandly to the upper floors as Theo, in a dinner jacket that sat superbly across his broad shoulders, turned from saying good night to the very last guest.

As he turned, his eyes rested on her for just a moment. And in that single moment she realised, with seismic shock, that she had been totally, completely wrong about him.

She could still feel the echo of that shock wave. Felt it resonate now, as she sat in the padded leather seat, gazing blindly out of the aeroplane window, heading back to Athens.

From that moment on, as that seismic shock had jarred through her, her marriage had changed for ever.

At first she had not believed it. She had assumed that in that moment when his eyes had rested on her with that expression in them she had been mistaken. She must have been mistaken. There was no other explanation. It had been late, she'd been tired, she had drunk wine—and so had he. That expression in them, therefore, had been nothing to do with her. Had been a recollection—or an anticipation. But not of her. Never of her. How could it have been?

Their marriage was a sham, a façade, a hollow charade. They had entered into it for no other purpose than to be exactly that. And until that moment he had treated her with complete and studied indifference. So how, *how* could that look possibly have been directed at her…?

But it had been—

And it had been unmistakable. Completely and absolutely unmistakable. A look as old as time. As clear as day.

Directly unambiguously, transparently—devastatingly—right at her.

A single look. Nothing more.

Nothing less.

And by it she had known, with a churning in her stomach, with a weakening of her limbs, a debilitating flush of betraying blood in her veins, that her fake, sham charade of a marriage had become something completely, absolutely different.

It had become a hunt.

She closed her eyes in worn, mental exhaustion, drawn back down into that inescapable past.

A hunt. That was what Theo Theakis had conducted. From that moment on, from that one single glance that had stripped away from her all the puerile illusions she'd had, she had become a hunted creature. Prey to a skilled, ruthless and unrelenting predator. A predator who had made her his target and kept her ruthlessly, remorselessly, in his sights.

His campaign had been so skilful. Slow, assiduous, bringing to bear all the expertise he had so abundantly at his disposal, honed to perfection on so many, many women. And she had been the focus of it.

As the days, weeks had followed, and Theo had slowly moved in for the kill, she'd realised that there was only one place that he was guiding her to, only one destination he had in mind for her—his bed.

CHAPTER SIX

LIKE a recording set to endless replay, Vicky again felt the hollowing of her insides that she had experienced when it had finally dawned on her just what Theo had in mind for her. And just as she had that time, she felt the same reaction—absolute blind panic.

Followed by absolute blind fury.

What the hell did he think he was doing?

That was what had screamed through her mind then. It still did now. But now, dear God, now she knew what she had not known then. That Theo Theakis was a man who would balk at nothing—nothing at all—to get what he wanted.

She felt her palms grow cold. God, she knew that all right! Her presence here, now, was terrifying, outrageous testament proof of that!

She heard his cold, chilling words echo in her mind.

'I want to finish what I started...'

She opened her eyes, staring ahead of her, blind and unseeing. In her ears Bach's convoluted intricate harmonies wove a universe of order and serenity. It mocked the raw, ragged torment in her mind.

I have to do this. And I can—I can do this.

Because I must...

And when she had—when she had done it—she would finally be done with Theo Theakis. For ever.

I'll have finished what he started—what I never, ever wanted him to start.

And then Theo Theakis could go to the hell he deserved.

Grim, dogged determination filled her, and a loathing of the man who was doing this to her crammed every cell of her body.

She felt the plane tilt, circle down, come into land, touch down, the jet engines screaming into reverse thrust to brake the plane, decelerate to a standstill.

Limply, she let her hand lie in her lap, then jerkily she unfastened her seat belt and looked around. Theo was already on his feet, and so was his aide. Theo did not look at her, simply headed for the exit, pausing to murmur brief thanks to the steward and stewardess, and acknowledge the pilot and co-pilot. Demetrious followed him, carrying his briefcase. He half hesitated, Vicky saw, as if to turn and speak to her, then simply hurried off after his employer.

It was the stewardess who came down to her to escort her from the jet. Theo was long gone, and Vicky knew why and was glad of it—even though she knew perfectly well that Theo had only been concerned about himself, not her. But at least it meant that she was spared what she had been dreading—being spotted by the paparazzi that hung around waiting for VIP passengers to come through.

If they knew I was back in Greece with Theo they would have a field-day!

She shivered involuntarily. Hadn't it been bad enough being an object of virulent curiosity to every woman who had had, or wanted to have, an affair with Theo? But on top of that she had also, thanks to her marriage, been an object of voyeuristic fascination to the Greek paparazzi, and to her consternation she had become used to the flash of photographs being taken whenever she went anywhere public with Theo, and often when she was on her own, as well.

A grim light glowered in her eyes. It had been the paparazzi, trailing her to that hotel, who had precipitated the vicious ending of her marriage...

She pulled her mind away. She would not let herself recall that hideous scene again, in which Theo had poured down on her all the savage fury he was capable of. Just as she would not, *would not*, let herself think about what she was doing now, returning to Greece.

A car was waiting for her, large, sleek and expensive, with tinted windows and a chauffeur. The moment she realised that that was to be her form of transport Vicky felt relief flush through her. The car indicated that she was staying on the mainland. God alone knew just how many beds Theo owned across his myriad properties, but there was one above all others that she dreaded.

No—no thinking of that. No memories allowed. Total shutdown of brain function—that was all that was allowed when it came to that subject.

Don't think—don't think about the island...

The island where she had endured her greatest ordeal.

Far more unbearable than the vicious savaging with which he had disposed of her as his wife.

Far more unbearable than that...

Cold snaked down her spine at the thought of Theo maximising his revenge by taking her back to that place...

But if she had been spared the island, where was he then intending to keep her? Pincers nipped at her insides. Was he planning on having her stay in the Theakis mansion? Please, no! It would be far too easy for her uncle to discover her presence there—

As ever, when she thought of Aristides, anger flushed

through Vicky. Theo had not spared her uncle either in his vicious savagery. He had destroyed her relationship with Aristides, her only living paternal relative, and she would not forgive him for that any more than she would forgive him anything else.

As the car started to leave the airport complex she saw it was not heading towards Athens, and the pincers in her stomach stilled. Nor were they heading for Piraeus, the port of Athens, so it was not to be his yacht, either.

So where, then?

It was as the car headed for the coast, and she made herself look at the road signs, that she finally realized. And when she did she felt a spurt of uncontrollable, furious anger.

She knew *exactly* where she was being taken!

Bastard! The absolute bastard!

Fury bit in her.

He was doing it on purpose—that was obvious. Making his point. Rubbing it in. Showing her, very visibly, what he intended to make of her! She felt her temper seethe. Then, out of her bile, another emotion emerged. The same one she had summoned last night, as she'd steeled herself to do what she had to do. This was a game two people could play. He thought he was calling the shots—well, he could think again!

He could damn well think again!

She had her own agenda for this hellish interlude, and she'd stick to it through thick and thin.

She sat back in the soft leather seat as the chauffeured car whisked her luxuriously to her destination. It did not take very long to get there, and she was not surprised. After all, it had to be a convenient distance from Athens. A quick enough run to fit in with the crowded agenda of a busy chief executive whose time was scarce and valuable.

'*Kyria?*'

The voice of the driver was impersonal, but his glance, as Vicky got out of the car at her destination, was less so. As she caught the discreet appraisal in his eyes, his expression of brief puzzlement only confirmed that she had been delivered to the correct place. Why else would Theo's chauffeur think it odd that he had just delivered a woman dressed in jeans and a cheap top to a place like this? The women who were brought here were light years away from her—they would never have worn chain-store clothes, or have been seen without a full face of make-up and hair done up to match. They would be svelte and chic and sophisticated, and above all always stunningly beautiful—the way Christina Poussos was.

And they would be preeningly gratified to be the object of his attentions. Even more gratified, Vicky knew, with another caustic glint in her eye as she surveyed her destination, to have been brought here.

Her eyes ran over the house in front of her. It had been built well off the main coast road, tucked discreetly away, far from prying eyes, deep in lushly watered gardens, surrounded by a high wall and the usual electronic security the wealthy found normal. It was small by the standards of the rich, not a mansion, but it was opulent and luxurious and Vicky knew exactly what sort of place it was.

She'd been told about it—but not by her husband. By a woman who had been at one time a guest here—'*Many* times, my dear'—so she had informed Vicky, with one of those sweetly insincere smiles she had become accustomed to. Vicky hadn't reacted—why should she have? It had meant nothing to her—and her blankness had clearly annoyed the woman.

She reacted with the same blankness now as she walked into the house, the door opened for her by a member of staff she had no reason to recognise from her marriage. The staff here would be quite different from those at any of the other Theakis properties in Greece—the vast mansion in Kifissia, the apartment in the city centre, the ski lodge in the mountains and the *faux*-primitive beach villa on the island.

Even if they did recognise her, it would not matter. The staff here, Vicky knew, would have been selected not just for their ability to be invisible, but primarily for their absolute and total discretion, blind and deaf to the identities of their employer's 'guests'. There would be no leaks to gossip columnists or paparazzi from these servants.

It was cool indoors, compared to the brief heat of the exterior between the air-conditioned car and the air-conditioned interior, and Vicky gave an unconscious shiver. It was the sudden chill that had made her shiver, she told herself. Nothing else.

With studied blankness she strolled forward, across the marble floored entrance hall and then into the shaded reception room beyond. It had been, she surmised, professionally designed for style and luxury, lacking any kind of personal touch. Through the slatted blinds she could make out a veranda, and the sea beyond.

Hefting her backpack to her other shoulder, she walked back out into the hall and headed upstairs. There was no sign of any more staff anywhere, but Vicky knew that if she dumped her backpack on the hall floor it would invisibly be taken upstairs at some point, and its meagre contents unpacked for her.

On the upper landing were several doors, and she opened one at random. It was a guest bedroom. The next was a bathroom as large as a bedroom. A small, scornful smile nicked her mouth, devoid of humour—with a sunken bath easily able to accommodate two people, plus a Jacuzzi and a walk-in shower. The next door opened to what must be the master bedroom, with a bed the size of her own bathroom.

She shut the door abruptly and returned to the first bedroom. That, at least, though still opulently decorated in the same professionally anonymous style of the downstairs décor, lacked a football pitch of a bed in which sleeping was obviously not the designated activity.

Like an automaton she crossed to the window, drawing up the blinds and staring out. She could see down over the gardens and the swimming pool to a small, private shingle beach, with a jetty to one side and the sea glinting with a blue that the colder shores of the UK never saw.

Emotion moved within her, and she slammed down on it. Her face set, she dumped her backpack on the bed and started to empty the contents over the counterpane. Unpacking would help to pass the time.

Stop her thinking.

That was essential. Quite essential.

But her unpacking took almost no time at all, and within minutes it was done. She glanced out of the window again. The shadows were lengthening; the two-hour time difference, plus the flight time, had eaten up the day. On a sudden impulse she lifted the house phone. It was answered immediately, and she issued a request for coffee to be served on the terrace. Then, armed with her book, she went downstairs.

The temperature on the terrace, despite the time of day, was still warm enough to make her wish she'd changed into more lightweight clothes. But if she'd done that she would have had to have a shower first, and she was in no mood to do that. It would have meant stripping off, seeing her naked body.

Her stomach plunged. Suddenly the reality of why she was here hit her all over again like a sledgehammer. She felt panic explode in her chest.

Oh, God, I can't do this! I can't! I can't!

Panic beat like a wild animal, and she could feel her heart rate leaping. Then, clenching her hands, she forced herself to calm.

Stop it—stop it right now. Ruthlessly she clamped down on

her burst of emotion. *You can do it—but the only way is to not think. Just don't think about what you're doing. That's all you have to do.*

That's all...

Grimly, she forced herself back into that state of deliberate blankness she'd managed before, sitting herself down on one of the padded chairs set out in the shade from which she could see the swimming pool, one end curved around into a whirlpool, with a set of waterproof switches inset into a stone slab at one end. She looked away and flicked open her book, making herself start to read. A few minutes later the coffee arrived. It was filter coffee, not Greek, and there was a plate of little Greek pastries and biscuits to go with it. She eyed them a moment. She ought to make herself eat something, she knew, because she'd been unable to eat on the plane, and breakfast had been an impossibility, too. But she contented herself just with sipping coffee instead.

Sip and read. Sip and read.

Don't think. Sip and read. Sip and read.

But thoughts came all the same. Threading into her brain between the words of her book, pooling like acid into her stomach.

She was here, in Greece. She had not been here for two years. All around she could hear the chitter of cicadas, feel the warmth of the southern clime, see the Mediterranean vegetation and the sparkle of the sun on blue, blue water. This time yesterday she'd had no idea at all that she would be here.

No idea of the ordeal ahead of her.

Am I mad to do this? Even to think I can do this?

Doubt assailed her, eroding what little dogged determination she was retaining. Disbelief swept over her, and then panic again, and she had to fight them both down.

I can do this—I can get through it, and I can come out the other side. And I will. That's exactly what I'm going to do. I'm

*going to come out the other side, and I'm going to get my
money, and then I'm going home—home to my real life. Home
far, far away from here—and farther away from Theo Theakis
than he can ever reach again.*

She felt anger and loathing for him pool deep within her.
She let it gather, taking strength from it. Let his image form
in her mind.

Tall, dark, deadly.

Abruptly she jumped to her feet, dumping her coffee cup on
the tray and letting her book tumble to the floor. She strode off
the terrace, past the pool, with its purpose-built whirlpool, and
plunged down the set of steps that led on to the shingle beach.
It was only a tiny beach, hardly enough to stride along. The
vegetation at either end was too thick for her to negotiate, and
she was reduced to crossing and recrossing the patch of shingle
as all around her the warm Mediterranean dusk gathered like
a thickening blanket, pierced only by the noise of the cicadas
in the foliage.

Agitation poured through her, a sick anxiety, as she strode
up and down, backwards and forwards, the soles of her trainers
crunching the gravel. Then, without knowing why, she halted.
Her skin seemed to prickle. She had heard nothing, but she was
spiked with awareness.

Slowly, very slowly, she turned to look back at the villa.

Theo was standing on the veranda.

Watching her.

Theo let his eyes continue to rest on her, even though she was
now aware of his presence.

She was agitated. That was good. It meant that the air of
blankness she'd pulled over herself during the flight had been
nothing but a pose. She was good at poses, he knew—all too
well. Posing at being his wife—until she'd been caught *in fla-*

grante by the gutter press who had, for once in their sordid, voy-euristic lives, come in useful.

A familiar fury gripped him—fury on so many, many counts. Fury at her sheer gall, at her daring to do what she had and then, when confronted with it, being without shame or repentance. Fury at her continued shamelessness, thinking she was entitled to the money Aristides had set aside for her, for which she had repaid him with dishonour and disgrace. But she hadn't cared about that, either. Or about anyone else…

Deliberately he let the fury drain out of him. It had had two years to drain out now, and there was no point letting it return. Emotion was out of place now. All emotion. He did not need to be Greek to know that the first rule of revenge held true whatever the nationality of the injured party. Revenge was a dish to be eaten cold.

It was a dish he would start to dine on tonight.

Abruptly he raised a hand, and summoned her to him.

Vicky went back up to the villa. She didn't want to. She wanted to find a power boat—a fast one—climb into it, let out the throttle and carve a way through the sea until the land behind was gone. Until Theo Theakis was gone.

But she couldn't. So instead, with steady tread, she walked up the steps and on to the veranda. She stood, saying nothing. Not meeting his eyes.

But punishingly aware of his physical presence.

For a moment he stayed silent. Then he spoke.

'Get changed. Clothes have been delivered for you. I'll meet you for drinks in an hour.'

She didn't deign to answer, just walked past him into the villa and out into the hall to go up the stairs. In the room she'd selected there were two people. One was a member of the house staff, and the other, she assumed, was some kind of personal shopper. They were placing clothes in the closet, on rails and in drawers.

'I'm going to take a shower,' Vicky announced, and went through to the bathroom, shutting the door firmly. Inside, she felt the bitterness starting to pool again. She took a sharp breath, stared dead ahead of her into the mirror above the vanity unit. But she did not meet her own gaze. She did not even look at herself. She looked at the reflection of the far wall in the glass. Then, counting to three, she steeled herself and started to pull her clothes off.

By the time she emerged a few minutes later she was clean, her hair towelled dry, swathed in a bathrobe. It was too skimpy on her, and she felt too much of her legs exposed. Both the other women were still in her room, clearly awaiting her. She forced a polite smile to her face, thanked them and dismissed them. She did not want anyone around while she dressed.

With a calmness she had to impose rigidly on herself she set to, sliding open drawers and sifting through the plastic-swathed clothes now hanging in the closet. It didn't take more than a few seconds to see exactly what instructions the personal shopper had been given. For a brief moment anger surged in Vicky. Then, with a grim tightening of her mouth, she reminded herself that that choice of attire suited her purposes entirely, as it happened. Whatever Theo's agenda was, she had one of her own. One that she must not waver from.

With iron discipline, stony-faced, she made her selection and started to get ready.

She hadn't brought a stick of make-up with her. But the personal shopper had seen to that, as well. A vanity case bearing the logo of a famous parfumier had been set out for her.

It took nearly all of the hour Theo had allocated her to do what she had to, and she did it with all the blankness she could summon to her aid. Then, with nothing more than a last, expressionless glance at her own reflection, she made her way downstairs.

He was in the reception room, and he was on his mobile. She walked in, crossed to the cocktail cabinet which had been opened to show a lavish display, and poured herself a vermouth. A large one.

Then she turned, glass in hand.

Her ex-husband had stopped talking.

Slowly, very slowly, he slid the phone back into his jacket pocket. Then he just stood and looked.

CHAPTER SEVEN

THEO could feel his body react. It would have been impossible for it not to have done. Emotions surged through him along with his body's animalistic response.

One emotion was obvious, but the other—

The other was completely out of place. He thrust it aside.

Then, like the connoisseur of fine women he was, he allowed his overriding sensation free rein—along with his eyes.

She was wearing eau-de-nil silk, clinging to her body more closely than her own pale skin, the material cupping her breasts and revealing their deep, exposed cleavage. Her fair hair was swept loose around one shoulder, falling seductively over one side of her face. Her eyes were huge in her face, lashes sooted with mascara, deepened by shadow, and her mouth was a lush curve of shimmering colour.

She stood, weight on one leg, one hand loose, the other raising a glass to her mouth. She took a slow, deliberate sip, then lowered the glass again. It was a calculated, provocative gesture.

So, he thought, that was how she was going to play this, was it? The mix of emotions clashed in him again, and, as before, he thrust aside the irrelevant one.

He knew what the woman in front of him was. He'd known it for a long time now, and it was not knowledge that drew from him anything other than the desire to do exactly what he was going to start tonight. The dish he was going to consume cold, and so very, very enjoyably.

He started to walk towards her.

Vicky stood, completely frozen, glass in her hand, like a rabbit that was being approached by a lean, intent predator. But beneath the frozen stillness of her pose something was running. Running in her veins, her nerves, her skin, like a fire through tinder-dry grass.

And it was tinder-dry all right.

Two years—two *years*—since that fire had last run in her veins.

Memory crashed through her, fusing present with past in a searing moment.

Theo, walking towards her, with one intention, one intention only, in his eyes, eyes that held hers, not letting her go, not letting her move.

Not letting her escape…

She'd wanted to—desperately—but she hadn't been able to. Hadn't been able to run, hadn't been able to move. Had only stood there while he walked towards her, reached for her…

He was reaching for her now, his hand fingering down the long fall of her hair beside her face. Hair was supposed to be unfeeling, and yet, if so, how was it that a million nerve-endings had started to fire within her?

For a long, endless moment he said nothing, just held her eyes, his eyelids lowering infinitesimally as he contemplated her. She stood immobile, quivering with awareness of him. Of his closeness.

Of his intent.

Then, in a gesture that was almost leisurely, he let his hand fall.

'Dinner first, I think,' he murmured.

He strolled through into the dining room that opened off the drawing room. Vicky followed behind. Her heart had started to thump. She tried to make it stop, but it wouldn't. So she took another mouthful of her vermouth. Its spiced headiness made her feel better.

Stronger.

And she needed to be strong. She needed to be absolutely strong.

One of the house staff was holding her chair, and she took it with a murmured thank you. It came out automatically in Greek, and the realisation made her uneasy. She didn't want to feel she was in Greece. Didn't want to do anything.

Except get this over and done with.

She cast a belligerent eye at Theo as he took his own place.

Why the farce of dining with me? Why not just lug me straight up to that ludicrous bed and do what you brought me here to do?

But she mustn't think about that—that was a bad idea, very bad. She took another mouthful of vermouth. Then, seeing that a glass of white wine was being poured for her, she seized that and drank from that instead. It didn't mix well with the vermouth, but she didn't care. She wanted the alcohol.

Needed it.

'If you're thinking of passing out cold on me, think again.'

Her eyes flashed to the far end of the table. Words rose in her mouth, words that would tell him that being out cold would be the best way of facing what he had in mind for her. But the presence of the staff, however impassive their expressions, stilled her. Instead, she made a show of pushing her wineglass aside in favour of the tumbler of sparkling mineral water that had also just been poured for her.

They ate in silence. It was difficult to do anything else while the staff hovered. Vicky wasn't sure whether she was glad they were there or not. Their presence kept a veneer of normality over the proceedings, but to her that only made it even more hypocritical.

How she got through the meal she did not know. Theo said nothing more to her, seemed preoccupied. And she did her best not to look at him. Nor to let herself think. Or feel. Feel anything at all. She must not, she knew. She must just sit there, lifting food to her mouth and lowering her fork again. Taking sips, repeatedly, of the wine poured for her by the silent, soft-footed staff who waited on them. Did they find it odd that their employer and his latest mistress sat and ate in complete silence? If they did, she didn't care—wouldn't care. God knew what they'd seen here in their time! She didn't want to think about it. Let alone imagine it...

Theo, with all his willing, willing women...

Well, not me! Not me!

Anger spurted through her. Then, like a house of cards, it collapsed.

A voice sliced into her head. Low, insidious, and so, so deadly.

Liar...

She stilled. Every muscle in her body freezing.

Liar, came the voice again, the one inside her head.

You were willing once...

In the end...

Of their own volition, drawn by a power she could not resist, her eyes went to him. She felt her breath catch in her lungs.

Why—why did it happen every time she looked at him? Because ever since she had first laid eyes on him she had felt it—felt his power. Power to disturb her. Dismay her.

And power to do much, much more to her. To make her do what she so did not want to do.

Her mind slid away to the past, the wine in her veins making it all too easy to do so, and memory suffused through her.

From the moment, so vivid still in her mind, when he had let his eyes rest on her as she stood at the foot of the stairs, and she had seen and felt his intent, he had hunted her down.

Relentless, purposeful, knowing what he wanted and set on getting it. Until, at the last, he had breached her resistance.

The island. How had she been insane enough to go there? She had thought it a refuge, a haven. A place where she could hide—escape. She should have known it was not that at all. That it was a trap, a lure, and once there she would have no place to run. No retreat.

She had fled there, to the private island Theo had mentioned in passing, never realising, in her stupidity, that she had done exactly what he had wanted her to do. Played right into his skilled hands. That the deliberate pressure he had exerted on her in the immediately preceding days, when he had racked up the tension so that she was incapable of rational thought, had all been part of his campaign.

The campaign had not been hurried or precipitate. No, it had started slowly, oh, so slowly, from that fateful initiation. A slow, deliberate process of letting her know, little by little, what his intentions were. Even when she had realised, disbelievingly, that she really was not misunderstanding the signs, that for some insane reason Theo Theakis thought he could enjoy her in his bed, he had continued.

I should have challenged him right there and then! Told him where to get off!

But she hadn't—little by little, week by week, he had worked on her. A look, an assessing regard, a flicker of awareness of her, the way he spoke to her, set his eyes on her. Until, finally vulnerable, trapped within the demands of her fake marriage with all the terrifying opportunities for an intimacy that had never, never been in the contract, he had turned on her the full force of the potency of his power and magnetism.

He had succeeded in making her weak and vulnerable—and gullible.

So gullible.

GET FREE BOOKS and FREE GIFTS
WHEN YOU PLAY THE...

777

Lucky 7

SLOT MACHINE GAME!

Just scratch off the silver box with a coin. Then check below to see the gifts you get!

YES! I have scratched off the silver box. Please send me the 2 free Harlequin Presents® books and 2 free gifts for which I qualify. I understand I am under no obligation to purchase any books, as explained on the back of this card.

306 HDL ELUX   **106 HDL EL2M**

FIRST NAME   LAST NAME

ADDRESS

APT.#   CITY

STATE/PROV.   ZIP/POSTAL CODE

7	7	7	Worth **TWO FREE BOOKS** plus 2 **BONUS** Mystery Gifts!
🍒	🍒	🍒	Worth **TWO FREE BOOKS**!
♣	♣	♣	Worth **ONE FREE BOOK**!
🔔	🔔	🍒	**TRY AGAIN!**

www.eHarlequin.com

(H-HP-07/07)

Offer limited to one per household and not valid to current Harlequin Presents® subscribers.

DETACH AND MAIL CARD TODAY!

© 2001 HARLEQUIN ENTERPRISES LTD.
® and ™ are trademarks owned and used by the trademark owner and/or its licensee.

The Harlequin Reader Service® — Here's how it works:

Accepting your 2 free books and 2 free mystery gifts places you under no obligation to buy anything. You may keep the books and gifts and return the shipping statement marked "cancel". If you do not cancel, about a month later we'll send you 6 additional books and bill you just $3.80 each in the U.S. or $4.47 each in Canada, plus 25¢ shipping & handling per book and applicable taxes if any.* That's the complete price and — compared to cover prices of $4.50 each in the U.S. and $5.25 each in Canada — it's quite a bargain! You may cancel at any time, but if you choose to continue, every month we'll send you 6 more books, which you may either purchase at the discount price or return to us and cancel your subscription.

*Terms and prices subject to change without notice. Sales tax applicable in N.Y. Canadian residents will be charged applicable provincial taxes and GST. All orders subject to approval. Credit or debit balances in a customer's account(s) may be offset by any other outstanding balance owed by or to the customer. Please allow 4 to 6 weeks for delivery.

BUSINESS REPLY MAIL

FIRST-CLASS MAIL   PERMIT NO. 717   BUFFALO, NY

POSTAGE WILL BE PAID BY ADDRESSEE

HARLEQUIN READER SERVICE
3010 WALDEN AVE
PO BOX 1867
BUFFALO NY 14240-9952

NO POSTAGE
NECESSARY
IF MAILED
IN THE
UNITED STATES

It had come to a head when, returning to Athens after nearly a week in Zurich on business, he had informed her that there was a gala ball to which they had been invited. It had been bad enough just realising that her heart rate had quickened discernibly when she had returned to the mansion and heard Theo's deep tones issuing instructions to one of the house staff. Worse when, hearing her arrival, he had emerged from his study, still wearing his business suit, and her lungs had squeezed out the air in them at the sight of him after a week. Had he seen her betraying reaction? With hindsight she knew he must have. He was far too experienced not to know. He had strolled forward, enquired after her health in a formal fashion, then reminded her of the hour at which they would have to leave that night.

The ball had been her worst ordeal yet. She had had to dance with Theo.

Of all things, a waltz.

She had been wearing a ballgown of red satin, strapless, with a high bodice that wrapped her torso tightly, gliding in to her waist then falling in a long, straight skirt to her ankles. A diamond and ruby necklace, one of the dozen items of similar jewellery that Theo had bestowed on her to wear for the duration of their marriage, had glittered at her throat, diamond and ruby drops at her earlobes. Her hair had been up, in a severe French pleat, and her make-up had been subtle and subdued.

Theo's eyes had narrowed very slightly, she recalled, as she had descended the staircase in the Theakis mansion, to where he waited, tuxedo-clad, in the hall below. As she'd come up to him, her expression impassive, she'd seen and been sure of it, a glint in his dark veiled eyes.

'Very English,' he observed, and the glint came again, making nerves flutter in her chest.

'Shall we go?' was all she said, and started towards the door.

Only the sudden pressure of her fingers on her satin evening bag betrayed her agitation.

All through their arrival and the early part of the proceedings Vicky managed to maintain her composure. Aristides was there, and she was glad of it, making a beeline for him when the sultry divorcee, Christina Poussos, who was clearly determined to resume her affair with him, commandeered him, shamelessly taking his arm and pressing her black-sheathed body against his as she led him away because he 'must meet' a most influential Argentinean financier.

But she was less glad of her uncle's presence when, after letting her chat to him for fifteen minutes, he said to her, with a mixture of indulgence and reproof, 'Go and rescue your husband from Christina Poussos before she thinks she can steal him from you, *pethi mou*!'

Vicky stifled an urge to say that Christina Poussos and her entire sisterhood could whisk him away any time they fancied, knowing she must say no such thing to Aristides. So she made her way to the cluster of people where Theo stood, his arm still held by the woman who, Vicky idly assessed, probably fell into the category of females whom Theo had once enjoyed, and had since replaced, but who had ambitions to return to his bed. Certainly the Greek woman's eyes glittered malevolently at Vicky as she arrived to join the group. But her reception by the middle-aged Argentinean was quite different. He broke off in mid-sentence to pay her a fulsome compliment, his eyes working hotly over her. Christina introduced her, and Vicky could almost hear her teeth gritting. Then, as the orchestra started to play, the other woman's eyes lit.

'Dancing at last! Theo, you know I love to dance!' She smiled flirtatiously at him before switching her gaze to the Argentinean. 'Enrique, take care of Victoria, won't you? Theo—' The flirtatious smile was back on her red-painted lips.

How it happened, Vicky did not know. Presumably with the same cool, ruthless skill and will that he brought to bear on everything. But the next moment Christina Poussos was disengaged from Theo, and her own hand taken. Then he was saying, in deceptively casual tones, 'The first dance must be with my wife, I think,' and she was being led out on to the huge dance floor as the orchestra swept into a waltz.

It had happened so fluidly she had no chance to realise his intention—and now it was too late.

She had been taken in his arms. His hand slid around her waist, resting lightly, firmly—immovably—in the small of her back, and his fingers laced through hers.

'Your left hand goes on my shoulder,' he murmured, glancing down at her.

Numbly, she did as she was bid, her feet starting to move as he impelled her forward. Her heart seemed to have gone from being frozen solid in her chest to lodging breathlessly in her throat.

They started to dance. And as they did Vicky understood for the first time in her life just why waltzing had once been considered scandalous.

She was so *close* to him! Closer than she had ever been! Held almost against him, her body posed and positioned by the subtle pressure of his hand splayed at her waist, his long, strong fingers laced through hers, and worst, worst of all, his lean, muscled thighs brushing against her skirts as he moved her backwards into the dance, turning her as he did so.

She gazed up at him—quite helpless. His face was so close to her, too—far, far too close. She could see the blade of his nose, the lines around his mouth, the firm outline of his lips, the smooth, freshly shaven jawline and more devastating yet, the dark glint of his eyes half veiled by thick black lashes.

And there was something more powerful still. Primitive potent. The scent of his masculinity, the faint spice of aftersh teasing at her. Her left hand rested as lightly as she dared on the smooth, expensive surface of his jacket, and through the fine material she could feel the sinewy muscles of his broad shoulders.

The music was haunting and rhythmic, old-fashioned but reaching deep, deep into her psyche, and they moved around and around, turning and turning on the dance floor, so that she could see nothing else, nothing at all except his lean, tanned face looking down at her, and her eyes locked to his—the only still point in a turning world. She was breathless, floating, caught and held, moving along the path that he set for her, guiding her, taking her where he wanted her to go...

Into a realm where only he existed for her.

And she gave herself to it as the music flowed in her limbs and her body. Helpless to do otherwise.

When, after an eternity, the music died, he stilled her, but her mind was whirling still, and all she could do was stand and gaze up at him, into his fathomless eyes.

And she recognised, deep, deep within her blood, what had happened to her. For one long endless moment she went on standing there, as all around couples were moving away, reforming, talking and laughing. She just stood there, trembling in every limb, and gazed at him, lips parted.

He looked down at her. Looked at her from his dark, dangerous eyes.

And smiled. The smile of a predator who had captured his prey at last...

She did not know how she got through the rest of the evening—had no recollection of it, no awareness. All her consciousness was focussed on one thing only.

She must escape.

Where—how—with what excuse? What reason?

It was during one of the distracted conversations she had during the course of that endless evening, when she made some

remark about how hot and breathless Athens was at the end of
September, that Aristides suggested the island Theo owned.

'It will be cooler there. Fresher than here. You should have
a holiday, both of you.' He beamed at them. 'You could go
there tomorrow!'

Vicky stiffened automatically, and Theo said, 'Impossible,
unfortunately. I can't get away until the weekend.' He glanced
at Vicky. 'You could go, however, and then I could join you on
Friday evening.' There was a bland look in his eyes, but Vicky
had seen the glint in them.

But all she murmured was, 'Very well.'

'Splendid!' Aristides exclaimed. He beamed at both of
them again.

Vicky forced a smile to her face. Oh, she would go to this
island, all right. But she would not be there, waiting like a
tethered goat, when Theo arrived at the weekend to finish off
his kill. She would be gone by then. Where, she didn't know
or care—but agreeing to go to this private island of Theo's
would buy her the precious time she needed. From there she
could make her own arrangements.

So she had gone. Like a fool, an idiot. Thinking she had
found a haven, a refuge from what she fled.

But Theo outmanoeuvred her effortlessly. She set off after
lunch, Theo safe in his offices in Athens. When she landed on
the island he was already there.

The island. Fragrant with the scent of thyme, cooled by the
breeze off an azure sea, a place of magic and enchantment. An
enchantment that sapped her will and lulled her senses even as
it awakened them.

When had the moment of yielding come? She did not know,
but it came all the same—a moment so silent, so imperceptible,
that she was not even conscious of it. As she walked up to the
tiny white-walled villa, framed by olive trees, splashed crimson

with bougainvillea, in all its bewitching simplicity, she felt her heart lift, her spirit lighten. Beyond the whiteness of the building she could see the cerulean blue of the sea, merging into the infinite sky above.

She felt a strange tranquillity steal over her, a sense of journey's end and resolution. Her pace slowed and she looked about her more deeply, drinking it in.

Then the sound of a door opening made her turn back towards the villa.

Theo stood in the doorway.

For one brief moment she stood, transfixed.

Waiting for the fury. The dismay.

But they did not come.

He held his hand out to her. He was not wearing his perpetual business suit. His short-sleeved shirt was open, the bronze of his chest darkened, his trousers nothing more than long swimming trunks, his feet bare, his hair feathered by the breeze. She felt desire shimmer in her. More than desire. Finally, more than desire.

There was nothing more she could do. She had fought, and run, and resisted.

But it had still come to this. She walked towards him and he looked down at her, took her hand, and led her in.

It was, in the end, all she could do.

Yield to him.

Why had she given in to him? Gone to his bed? Let him do to her what she had fought so hard against? She knew the truth of it—because she had not had the strength to go on resisting him. That was all.

He had sensed his victory from the moment she had walked up to him, and from that moment on she'd been lost. It had been as if all the fight had gone out of her—and he had known it. He'd said nothing of that, however, simply greeting her as if it had all been prearranged by both of them.

Maybe it had been the remote beauty of the island, their isolation, with no one else there once the helicopter that had brought her from the mainland had whirred off into the sky, letting the peace crowd back again into the silence.

'Come down to the beach,' Theo had said, taking her small suitcase and carrying it into the single bedroom. A simple room—whitewashed walls, stone floor, an old-fashioned bed, wooden furniture and slatted blinds.

Not a room for Theo Theakis—head of a mighty corporation, corporate captain *par excellence* and one of Greece's richest men.

And yet, as Vicky watched him curiously, he seemed at home here.

As did she. That was the strangest thing of all—the way she simply accepted what had happened, abandoned her fight. Let herself be taken over by him at last, to spend a lazy, easy day together on the beach, in the water, in the sun and the shade, letting the island work its strange, alluring magic on her, and then, as night fell, eating simple food, cooked by themselves in the low-tech kitchen, sitting at a rustic wooden table set out under the olive trees, drinking wine while the stars burned golden holes in the patches of the sky between the silvered olive leaves.

What they talked of she did not know, for another conversation was taking place, running silently between them, weaving their eyes together, until at last Theo rose to his feet, took her hand, and took her to his bed.

In the early morning, as he lay asleep beside her, she got up and dressed, and phoned from her mobile for the helicopter.

And fled.

CHAPTER EIGHT

MEMORY twisted inside her like a garrotte around her throat. She gazed now, down the length of the table, at the man who was going to wreak his revenge on her for what she had allegedly done to him.

Gone from his bed into another man's arms.

She'd had no idea—none—that she had been photographed with Jem at the airport where she'd met him, or that she had been trailed leaving with him as she fled. No idea at all until, three days later, knowing she could put it off no longer, she had returned to the Theakis mansion.

To be eviscerated by Theo's savage fury and thrown from her marriage in bloodied rags.

Never to be spoken to again, never to have her existence acknowledged—until now. When he had decided it was time for a little exercise in revenge...

Her eyes darkened. Revenge for her having committed the greatest crime of all, in his eyes—preferring another man to him.

That was all it was...

All it could possibly be. Their marriage had not been real, had been a sham, simply for show, so how could there even be a question of adultery?

No one even saw those photos! Only him!

So how could he have grounds for anger? Her mouth twisted. Was it just about the money it had cost him to buy them from the photographer who had, so Theo had hurled at her in that nightmare exchange, thought he could make more money by selling them to him rather than the newspapers? Well, so what? Theo Theakis had more money than he knew what to do with, and she wasn't responsible for the ludicrous interest the press took in him and his affairs!

He shouldn't have so damn many himself if he doesn't want the press all over him!

Well, she thought balefully, no one was going to find out about the 'affair' he was having right now, that was for certain.

With his own ex-wife.

She gazed down the table again, reaching automatically for her glass of wine. She wished she could pass out cold. Wished she could simply shut her mind, completely and totally, to what was going to happen. But she couldn't. She felt her stomach tighten. She had to do his. For Theo, it might be about revenge for his injured conceit about himself, but for her, oh, for her it was for a quite different reason.

Her eyes rested on him with tight deliberation, and she set down the glass again. She felt the wine wind into her blood-stream like a slow coil of satin, gliding over her nerve-ends subtly, so subtly, easing into the cells of her body. With the fringes of her mind she knew it was taking effect.

She looked about her, eyes drifting around the dining room. It was opulent, like the rest of the house, decorated in that same rich, uniform style—a setting, nothing more, for the true purpose of the house: to provide a discreet, luxurious place where sexual congress could take place with absolute privacy.

It was a house that had seen a great deal of such activity…

A pinched look haunted her eyes for a moment. Then she dispelled it. Her gaze went on drifting around, looking anywhere, everywhere, but at the man sitting at the head of the table.

Yet she could sense his presence as if it were solid. It was impossible not to. She was quiveringly, pulsingly aware of him with every beat of her blood. Finally, she lifted her eyes to do what she had refused to do all through the endless meal. Look down the long table to the man who wanted to take his revenge on her. A vengeance she had no choice but to let him take. No choice at all.

Starting right now.

In slow motion her gaze slid through the space between them and locked to his.

It was instant. Tangible. Physical. His eyes held hers as surely as if his hands had caught her. It was like being speared, caught and held, like a fish on a line. For a fraction of a second she wanted to pull away, but he would not relinquish her, and even as she tensed she felt the dissolution in her veins as she gave herself up to the leash on which she was being held. He had felt her moment of yielding. She could see it in the minutest relaxation of his face. He knew that she would not break the gaze between them, knew that he could go on holding her eyes with his, making her the recipient of the slow, probing exploration of his look. She saw the lines around his mouth begin to deepen into a smile—a smile of satisfaction.

Anticipation.

She got to her feet. Still without unlocking her gaze, she picked up her wineglass and took one last mouthful. Slowly she lowered the glass, but kept it between her fingers. Then, with the same slow movement, she turned away and walked towards the door.

Her hips were swaying, she could feel it through the line of her legs, her feet in their high heels. She could feel the fall of her hair rustle over her bare shoulder.

Feel his eyes follow her every step.

At the door she did not pause or turn. One of the staff was there before her, opening the door for her, but she did not acknowledge it. This was not the moment for other people. This was the moment only for her—and the man who would any moment now push back his chair and follow her.

She crossed the hall, her footsteps loud on the marble, and began to ascend the stairs. The wineglass was still in her hand and she paused halfway. She didn't need this now. She could feel its power already creaming in her veins like a silken veil.

As she moved she felt the sleek material of her dress move against her body, like a whispered caress over her skin. She could feel her body, feel its contours, feel the heat flushing slowly through her flesh as she made her swaying ascent. She paused at the landing, and then made her languorous way to the bedroom. The master bedroom.

The mistress bedroom.

Well, that was, after all, exactly what she was about to become. One of Theo Theakis's mistresses. One of so many. Enjoying with him an affair that was sensual, sophisticated and entirely pleasurable.

Just right for a mistress.

And therefore, with immaculate logic, entirely appropriate for her now...

So, now that she was to become Theo Theakis's mistress, she must do only what a mistress would do in these circumstances. Be only what a mistress would be.

Feel only what a mistress would feel.

Pleasure. Nothing but pleasure. Sensual and sophisticated and above all untainted by emotion. Quite, quite untainted by anything so completely unnecessary...

As she walked in, still with the same slow, undulating walk, she left the bedroom door open behind her. Moving towards the vast bed, she drew back the pristine counterpane and pressed the light switch to illuminate the room with a soft, flattering light. Then she slipped off her sandals and lowered herself down on to the bed. She posed herself carefully, languidly, one arm stretched out over her head, which lifted her breasts, the other hand splayed on her thigh, her legs slightly crooked. She could feel the hem of her dress, taut and high across her upper legs, feel the mounds of her breasts strain against the silky material covering them so skimpily.

She felt ripe and wanton.

And quite, quite alien.

But that was good. It was fine.

More than fine.

Necessary.

I can do this—I must...

The last echo of her mantra sounded in her head, then faded away, quite away.

She did not need the mantra any more. The ripe, wine-laden wantonness of her body was all she needed.

Right now, at this moment, as she lay arranged in her deliberate, knowing pose, her breasts full, her skin warmed and lustrous, deep within the slow heat building, it was all she wanted...

There was a shadow by the door—a dark presence electrifying her senses.

He was there. Coming towards her. His gait steady, purposeful. His features taut. His eyes—

Dark, so dark. Intense.

Intent, so very, very clear, on one purpose only...

She felt her breath catch, felt the shiver of what she knew—welcomed and rejoiced—was raw sexual excitement. The wine that filled her veins was had been replaced by this new feeling, and she could feel it absorbing into her consciousness. Nothing mattered except this moment, this sensuous, voluptuous *now*. The *now* that filled her, possessed her—changed her.

He came up to her. He was still formally dressed, and the sight of him in his business suit, with his broad shoulders moulded by the superb tailoring, the glimpse of the grey silk lining of his jacket, the pristine whiteness of his shirt stretched across his chest, slashed by the expensive discreet silk of his tie, made her feel, with a shiver of that same raw, sexual excitement, the full frisson of his power.

For a long moment he looked down on her, and she was what he saw—a woman displayed for him—beautiful, willing, and waiting for him. A mistress…

Some last, frail shadow of herself haunted the recesses of her mind, but it died away. She simply lay there, her sensuous pose displaying her, as his eyes worked leisurely along the languorous length of her supine body.

He sat down beside her, and she felt the mattress dip beneath his weight. He contemplated her one moment longer, without touching her. He said nothing, and nor did she. There were no words to say. This was not about words. This was about the fire in her blood, making her someone quite, quite different.

A mistress. The woman he wanted her to be.

The woman she now was for him.

And she would be that woman, willingly, wantonly, letting him, as he did now, reach a hand towards her face, letting his thumb graze sensuously along the lushness of her lip. His touch dissolved into her, and with a movement she could not stop she bit slowly, softly, into the hard pad of his grazing thumb, letting her tongue ease along it.

She saw the deep flare in his eyes, fathomless eyes, framed with long, impenetrable lashes. She bit softly again.

His thumb left her mouth, travelled slowly down the curve of her jaw, the line of her throat, pausing in the hollow at its base to feel the pulse with its slow, insistent beat. His hand moved on, palming over her bare flesh, fingers dipping into her cleavage, and then, with a considered, leisurely movement, he drew down the bodice of her dress to display her breasts to him.

Heat pooled between her legs. Her breath caught in her throat. She lay, breasts bared, while he drifted the tips of his fingers across them. He did not look at her, only at her breasts, and she felt them engorge and fill, their peaks flowering like exquisitely sensitive buds. The touch of his nails on them, so light, so devastating, dissolved her spine.

For a little while he continued to caress her breasts, almost in an exploratory way, seeing what his touch would do to them. She felt her fingers clench as sensation after sensation shot through her.

She could not think; she could only feel. She was only this— an exquisite net of sensation, playing through her body. Tiny shoots of fire laced from her nipples through the taut swell of her breasts, racing down, down the length of her abdomen, to feed the heat pooling between the vee of her legs.

Her lips parted and she gave a low, soft moan.

As if it were a signal, he moved with sudden swiftness, sliding one hand beneath her shoulder and turning her over with effortless strength, before she even realised what he was doing. The room swirled and settled, and then, with another, deeper shiver of excitement, she felt his hands smooth along the silk of her short skirt, riding up over her thighs. He smoothed the material upwards, ruching it towards the small of her back.

Exposing the bare mounds of her bottom.

She wore no panties. What would have been the point? They would only have had to be removed.

She felt him still. He had not expected that, for her to be so naked. She knew it deep inside her, where the heat was pooling, and the knowledge made her feel even more wanton. Her cheek was pressed against a pillow, her hands reaching up above her, fingers pressing into the edge, while the taut silk of her dress cut across the bared flesh of her bottom, displayed for his view.

Sensation surged through her. She felt arousal—full-on, incredibly erotic—flood her. Instinctively she stretched her spine, indenting her body into the mattress, her thighs falling very slightly apart.

'Don't move.'

The instruction was a low rasp, and she felt the mattress tilt again as he stood up. He was stripping his clothes off, she could tell, hearing the sound of rapidly discarded garments. Then there was the sound of a drawer in the bedside unit being pulled roughly open. There was a pause. She did not look. She knew what he was doing.

What he was preparing for.

She felt her heart rate increase, flushing through her veins, heating her yet more. Then, abruptly, the bed dipped again, but now the balance was different. Now she felt strong, muscled thighs either side of hers.

He was caging her, kneeling over her legs as she lay, displayed and semi-naked for him. She pressed her groin into the bedding again, feeling that incredible surge of erotic sensation, knowing what he was seeing. Her hands kneaded at the pillow.

Hunger filled her. Hunger and need. Displaying herself was not enough. She wanted more…much, much more. She stretched her spine again, minutely lifting her half-bared bottom to him. Inviting him.

He took the invitation. Hands curved hard over her, and pleasure flooded her. The tips of his fingers were beneath the silk hem of her dress, and his thumbs—his thumbs were dipping into the cleavage between the mounds of her bottom. Dipping and dragging, down, down, into the hidden valley between her thighs.

It was unbearable, incredible, so fantastically arousing that she lifted her head and shoulders, straining the curve of her spine.

A moan broke from her, and from him a soft, satisfied laugh.

For countless blissful moments he toyed with her, and then, in another sudden movement, his hands were at the zip of her dress. He unzipped it, hoisted her off the bed with a single sweep of one strong forearm around her waist, and peeled the dress off her completely, shucking it away down her legs and discarding it on the floor.

She was completely naked.

He flipped her over.

Her eyes went to his instantly, her hair tumbled around her face, lips parted. Her nipples were swollen aching peaks, her hands helpless and limp beside her head.

He caged his body over hers, his fingers sliding between hers, holding her, holding her exactly where he wanted her to be. Which, right now, was the only place in the entire universe where she wanted to be.

For a moment, a brief, slicing moment, disbelief consumed her. Then it was gone, gone completely, like a drop of cool water on a sizzling hotplate. Heat flared in her, excitement and arousal. There was only this—now, here. Lying aroused and pleasured, caged and waiting—waiting for what she wanted now, right now, right now…

Her eyes locked to his, challenging him, inviting him.

His body was so powerful, the bare muscled chest honed and sleek, every plane and muscle taut—and she wanted it. She wanted to feel its hard weight pressing her down, feel its strength, its rampant, urgent desire for hers. Wanted to feel that long, strong shaft fill her, thrust up into her, again and again and again, and she didn't want to wait—she didn't want to wait one moment more.

Her spine arched, and she strained her hands against his grip.

His thighs were pressing against hers, and she strained against them, lifting her hips to him.

'What are you waiting for, Theo?' she said, and her voice was a challenge, a husk, her eyes twining with his, writhing like twisting ropes. 'This is what you want, isn't it? It's what I'm here for, isn't it? To finish what you started—'

She lifted her hips again, her breasts rising, thrusting forward as she moved. Raw, urgent excitement, erotic and sensual, overrode everything, blotting out everything else.

It was just her body and his. And she wanted only one thing. She wanted it so, so badly...

He gave it to her.

With slow, taunting control he lowered himself down, sliding into her in one single, fluid movement.

She gasped, and threw her head back, sensation exploding in her. Oh, God, it was good! It was so, so good! She lifted to meet him, lifted against his thrust, wanting him to thrust again, right up to the very neck of her womb, as her muscles tightened around him. She was on fire, urgent, hungry, as hungry as a vampire scenting blood.

He thrust again, hard and hot, and she cried out, a sharp, high sound. Her fingers wound in his, every muscle clenched tightly in her body as she arched up to meet his scything downstrokes. Her spine sweated, her body was jerking, as the hard, relentless thrusts came again and again. Her body was melting, melting all around him, as if it was turning into something else, something that was hot, liquid metal, searing with heat, glistening with absolute, total arousal.

She could see his face and it was taut, intense. He was caught up in his own consuming pleasure as he scythed into her, hard, insistent, over and over again. And with every thrust the hot, metallic liquid that was her body came closer and closer and closer still to the moment she was gasping for with every urgent rasp in her straining throat. The moment that was almost, *almost* there, with every hard stroke against the inflamed, distended flesh inside her, that incredible spot she had heard about but never, never…

Sensation sheeted through her, a pleasure so powerful she could not believe it, crying out with a high, unearthly sound as every cell in her body fused into molten silver. And as they fused she seemed to feel his arms tighten convulsively around her, holding her so close against him that she could feel the hectic beating of his heart against hers. Something seemed to take her over, flooding through her, something that was nothing to do with the intensity of physical pleasure consuming her. Something that seemed to take her out of her own pulsing body, soaring upwards, higher and higher. An emotion so powerful that she could feel her arms wrap around the body in her arms as if it were the most precious thing in the universe…

No! The cry was silent, anguished. Theo wasn't precious to her—he was just a highly skilled sexual partner exerting his formidable expertise to ensure she got the maximum pleasure from his body.

That was all he was.

All this was.

Desperately her body arched and bucked, and she jerked her hips upwards, again and again, to keep that incredible pleasure going. Because she never, never wanted to lose it. She wanted to keep it, ride it, hot and greedy, wanting more and more and more of it. Because it was essential—essential she did not lose it, that she clung to it, fused with it, became one with it. Because if it started to fade, if it started to ebb, it would be, it would be…

It was fading. Ebbing.

Panic took her. She thrust up her hips, again and again, but there was nothing there, nothing to thrust herself against, no hardness, no fullness. And as the dawning recognition of that, and the reason for it, came to her, so, welling up in her like cold, icy water, came something else—something she could not, must not, *must* not, let into her mind.

But it came all the same. Seeped in on the cold, icy water that was filling her veins now, replacing the hot, greedy pleasure she had sated herself on, which had faded now, ebbed away. Leaving her on the bleak, bare shore, bereft of all sensation.

Bereft of everything.

Except one thing.

The knowledge of what she had just done.

She shut her eyes. It was instinctive, imperative. As if by refusing to see there would be nothing to see. Nothing to know. Nothing to feel.

But feel she must. She could not escape.

Her body ached. Ached from being distended, strained. Ached from the overloading of her sensory capacity.

He drew out of her. She could feel it—feel him unclasping her hands, which went on lying there limply, her whole body flaccid, collapsed. She kept her eyes tight, tight shut. They burned beneath the lids.

Her body felt cold, so cold.

What have I done?

The question coiled in her brain.

What have I done?

But she knew. She knew the answer. She had done what she knew she would have to do. Unfinished business, Theo had called it. He was right.

'Open your eyes.'

His words cut through her coldness.

She forced her eyes open. He was looking down at her, and his eyes were colder than she had ever seen them before in her life.

'Don't play your tricks with me again—not if you want your money. Understand?'

Then he was gone, walking into the en suite bathroom, shutting the door. She heard the shower start to run. Slowly, very slowly, she pulled the bedclothes over her.

A stone, hard and painful, blocked her lungs.

Theo's hands curved tightly around the steering wheel of his car, and he pressed his foot down on the accelerator. The low, lean vehicle sprang forward with a throaty roar. Gravel crunched under its tyres as he headed down the drive, opening the gates with a flick of an electronic switch and turning out on to the road beyond, dimly lit by a tired, waning moon.

He drove fast. But not fast enough to outrun his memory. Hot, pulsing memories of the sex he had just had.

Black emotion filled him. A dish eaten cold? No, it had been scalding, molten hot! His mouth thinned. She'd tried to turn the tables on him, manipulate him. Call the shots.

He'd let her do it—this time.

This time—deliberately, knowingly—he'd gone along with her. Let her play the vamp, lure him upstairs, set the pace. He'd chosen to let her do so, wanting to see just what she would do.

And now he knew. *Theos*, now he knew!

It had taken all his strength—all of it—to get out of there the way he had.

Leave her the way he had.

When every burning instinct had wanted to keep him there…

Cold snaked down his back. What had happened in his moment of white-out had been nothing, *nothing* of what he'd intended.

It was just a reflex—nothing more. Nothing more than that.

Or an illusion. He hadn't really felt her heart beat against his. Her arms tighten around him like that.

Deliberately he forced a hard, contemptuous smile to his lips. It had been just another trick of hers, that was all. One of the repertoire of tricks she'd tried out on him all evening, showing him her true colours, as he had known them to be since the moment he had seen those damning, condemning photos and discovered the truth about her

His hands clenched on the driving wheel as he pressed down yet harder on the accelerator, cutting through the night, back towards Athens.

He knew what she was. He didn't need to know anything else about her.

And what he knew about her damned her. Damned her completely.

The way she'd been tonight only confirmed it—as if he'd needed any such confirmation about just what kind of woman he'd married. Victoria Fournatos was as shameless as she was adulterous, and she deserved no quarter. None.

And that was exactly what she'd get from him.

It was all she deserved.

He drove on, into the blackness of the night.

But he would be back. Oh, he would be back, all right. He hadn't finished with her yet.

Not by a long way.

And next time he would stay absolutely, totally in control

It was essential he do so. Quite, quite essential.

He came again to her the following night. She was wearing a different dress this time. Red, with a halter neck and a short, swirling skirt. This time he did not dine with her. He'd eaten at a business dinner in Athens. She was sitting in the lounge, with the air-con on too high, watching an English language news channel.

As he walked in her eyes veiled immediately. She stood up.

Tonight she was different. She stood passive, not displaying her body, just standing there, not meeting his eyes, not posing as she had been last night.

Her passivity lasted the entire encounter. He took her

upstairs, turning her around in the bedroom to unzip and remove her dress. She was wearing panties this time, little wispy things that made him instantly hard. He stripped off his own clothes rapidly, and took her over to the bed.

She lay quite still while he reacquainted himself with her breasts. Only their physical response to his caresses told him that she was becoming aroused. That and the parted lips through which her breath was coming in soft, quick breaths, and the blind, glazed look in her eyes.

His hands made a leisurely progress, stroking and teasing until her nipples were hard and coral-red, his eyes always watching her body's reaction to him. Then, when he judged her sufficiently aroused, he let his hands slide downwards.

She was wet already, the delicate tissues plumped and swollen. He let his fingers glide in their satin folds, watched her bite her lip, the blind, glazed look becoming more unseeing. Her fingers, lying inert on either side of her, bit into the softness of the bed. A low, helpless moan escaped her constricted throat.

He moved over her.

This time he controlled the pace. Controlled it absolutely. He parted her thighs and paused at the entrance to her body. Then he began to inch himself into her, his control total. He saw her eyes flare, and when he had filled her completely knew that her pupils were at maximum dilation.

Then he began to move in her, slowly, skilfully, building a rhythm, his body under his complete control. Her body, too.

With the same absolute control he gave her her first orgasm, and then, as it subsided, he gave her a second. Each time he watched her skin flush, her breath freeze, felt her heart rate burst, felt her internal muscles flux wildly, drawing him in yet more deeply. Each time he let her subside, let the sweat dew on her body, the pulse at her throat slow down again.

Only then, finally, did he take her one last time, with himself, to that same point of sensation.

Only then, in his own pleasure, did he stop watching her.

When he had climaxed he left her immediately.

He could not bear to be in the same house as her.

Let alone the same bed…

Vicky lay, staring upwards. The ceiling seemed to be revolving. It was an illusion, she knew, caused by the fire in her bloodstream.

She lay unseeing as the room moved around her. She was still in the same position he had left her in. She had not moved a muscle. He had gone some time ago, walking out of the room fully dressed, not looking at her. She had been spared that, at least.

But nothing else.

Nothing else at all.

Revenge—that was what he wanted, and that was what he was taking. But for her it was something different.

It was exactly what he had planned for her.

Humiliation.

Cold ran through her, and a despair so deep within that she did not know where it came from.

It wasn't supposed to be like this!

How—how had it gone so wrong? She had been so sure that she could do it—could be exactly what she had to be in order to take from this what she needed to take.

I was going to turn the tables on him—not let him do what he wanted to me—humiliate me and take his revenge on me. I was going to be exactly the kind of woman he likes—sexually sophisticated, dedicated to sensual pleasure, wanting nothing more from him than physical sensation. I was going to stay in control and call every shot.

Instead he had turned the tables back on her. Seen through her pathetic attempt to resist him. To retaliate against him.

And now resistance and retaliation were impossible.

Now… Her eyes bleached with despair. Now there was only survival.

Getting through to the end.

Fear bit into her, like a stab in the belly. When would the end come? She had never bothered to ask just how long Theo intended her to stay here, because what would have been the point? He might not have told her, and it would simply have shown him how much she longed for the ordeal to be over. And that in itself would have given him a satisfaction she would never, ever willingly grant him.

But how long would he keep her here? How many nights had she still to endure?

Her fingers clutched into the sheets. There was nothing, nothing she could do. She would endure as long as she had to endure. Until Theo had finally finished with her.

Because only then would she, too, be finally finished with him…

Whatever the price she had to pay to do so.

Night after night he came to her. In the daytime, when the bright sun beat down, she was like an automaton. She got up, ate breakfast on the veranda, sat and read, swam in the sea from the shingle beach, up and down, back and forth, over and over and over again. She ate lunch and read. Drank coffee. Watched the sea, its tireless constancy marking the sameness of her days.

Then, by night, she went upstairs to her bedroom and adorned herself for Theo Theakis.

Every night he came and took her to his bed, gave to her body a physical pleasure that she could not bear to remember, either in the light or the dark, and then, when it was over, he left.

Leaving her slowly bleeding from wounds she could not stanch.

On the seventh night he emerged from the bathroom, fully clad in his business suit once more, and placed a piece of paper on the bedside unit.

'Your money,' he said. Then he walked out.

CHAPTER NINE

VICKY sat in the bed, looking at the piece of paper in her hand. The money she needed. The money she had come to Greece to get.

Well, she had it now

She went on staring at the piece of paper, with the curtly written signature on it, the zeroes of the figure in the box.

She could hear the sound of him walking down the stairs, out of the door, his monstrous car revving loudly, then swirling away down the drive—away, away, away.

When she could hear him no more she slowly placed the cheque back on the side table, then lay down, drawing the bed-clothes over her. She should sleep, she knew. Tomorrow she would be taken back to the airport, put on a plane, despatched to London. To get on with her life. And she could, now. She had her money, after all.

Think of the future. Think of when you start helping Jem restore Pycott. Think of the work ahead and the things to achieve. Think of the first schoolchildren arriving, the new hope they will have. Think of that. Think only of that.

Don't think about anything else.

You've got the money—be glad of that at least.

Closure.

That was the word, the word psychologists used to describe how essential it was for people not to have things hanging over their head emotionally. Closure to seal one part of life from another. The past from the present. The present from the future that was yet to come.

She had come for closure, but for her there could be no closure—not yet.

What Theo had done to her in his bed ensured that.

Instead of closure, something else was swelling inside her—something powerful, unstoppable. Something that was seeping through her, blotting through all her body.

And she knew exactly what it was.

And exactly what she was going to do about it.

She was packed and ready to go by eight in the morning. She had slept eventually, a heavy, dreamless sleep, and now she was calm, very calm, and that was good. As she painted on her face her hand did not tremble. When she was done she eyed herself objectively. Her full face of make-up did not go with the casual clothes she was wearing, but that didn't matter. She wouldn't be wearing them for long. They would not be suitable for her purpose.

Before she set off downstairs she checked her wallet one last time. Yes, the cheque was still there. She gazed at the dark, incisive handwriting, the strong scrawl of his signature. For just a moment she felt the emotion that had started to build up in her last night lash out, but she leashed it back in.

Not yet.

Soon.

She stood up, lifted her backpack, and headed out of the room. Along the corridor the shut door of the master bedroom looked back at her blankly. As blank as her own expression. Downstairs she took her leave of the staff, not looking any of them in the eye. She didn't like to behave like that, but for her own sanity she knew she had to. Then she walked out to the waiting car. The warmth after the perpetual air-conditioned cool of the interior made her shiver—or something else did. She looked back at the house.

A love-nest. That was the coy expression that used to be in vogue. Well, nothing to do with love had happened in there this week.

She shivered again, and got into the car. But as it started to move off she leant forward.

'I'm going into Athens,' she said to the driver.

He nodded, incurious, and she leant back.

It was strange, very strange, to see Athens again, to sit in one endless traffic jam after another and catch glimpses of the familiar outline of the Acropolis crowned by the Parthenon. Even though she did not want to, she felt herself react. Felt emotion start to run in her veins. She stopped it because she could not allow herself to do otherwise.

And because it was the wrong emotion.

There was only one emotion she was allowing herself now. Only one that was right and proper for the occasion.

Her first port of call was the bank. She'd opened her own account before they'd married, arranging to have funds placed there from her own British bank account in London. It was irrelevant that her uncle would happily have bankrolled her, and that as Mrs Theakis Theo had opened a separate account for her at his bank. She trusted only her own bank, her own name.

It did not take long to pay in the cheque Theo had left for her. But paying it in did not achieve the closure she needed. She had known it would not. Not now. Something much more was needed.

For that, she would need an outfit. One that suited the face she wore and the sleek styling of her hair. She ordered the driver to deposit her at the premises of one of the designers she had most favoured when she was Mrs Theo Theakis. The vendeuse was new, and she was grateful, but she kept her dark glasses on all the same. Nor did she linger over her decision, emerging less than fifteen minutes later wearing a classic shift dress in mint-green, with an off-white handbag and sandals to match. As she left the shop she took one last glance at herself in a full-length mirror.

She gave a small, tight smile to her reflection. Oh, yes, Mrs Theo Theakis was back in town all right!

And she wanted more than the money she was owed. Much more.

Now it was her turn for vengeance. And she would make sure it really, really hit Theo where it hurt. In his giant-sized masculine sexual ego.

Back in the car, she phoned his office. The voice that answered was familiar—it was Theo's aide, Demetrious. Vicky spoke crisply in English.

'This is Mrs Theakis here. Put Theo on the line, please.'

There was an imperceptible pause. Then, 'One moment, please, Mrs Theakis.' The aide's voice was as neutrally incurious as it had been on the flight over. He came back on the line a moment later.

'Mrs Theakis, I'm so sorry. Mr Theakis is in conference.'

The voice was smooth—apologetic, even—but Vicky knew that it was pointless to repeat her request. This time around was not going to be an action replay of her vigil in Theo's London offices. This time *she* was calling the shots. Starting right now.

'Oh, dear,' she answered. 'That's a pity. Would you let him know I'm going to be lunching at Santiano's, if he'd like to join me there? Thank you so much. I'm in the car at the moment, so he can reach me on that number.'

She hung up and sat back as the car continued to wind its way round Athens' infamously traffic-laden streets. Santiano's was the biggest hotbed of gossip in Athens. Everyone who wanted to be seen went there, and it was a favourite haunt both of gossip columnists and the paparazzi, waiting to see who was lunching with whom. And, of course, a lot more than lunching…

If the former Mrs Theakis was seen there, back in Athens, tongues would start to wag straight away. Even without the slightest shred of evidence the columnists would be speculating on whether she was going to be getting back with Theo Theakis again. A momentary pang went through her—if Theo called her bluff, then it was inevitable that Aristides would find out that she was back in Athens. She didn't want him hurt—not any more than he had been already.

But that was thanks to Theo anyway, she reminded herself mercilessly. There had been no need for Theo to tell Aristides why he was going for a divorce. No need to upset him the way he had, by telling him about those incriminating photos! He could just as easily have trotted out the story they had agreed they would tell her uncle all along—that the marriage had simply not worked out, and they were parting amicably.

Amicably…

Vicky felt her stomach hollow.

No, amicable their parting had *not* been.

Fierceness filled her again.

It's Theo's fault—it's all Theo's fault! I never asked for any of this—none of it! And I didn't deserve it! I absolutely did not deserve it. Even if I had—

The phone in the car went.

For a moment she let it ring, feeling her stomach hollow out. Then she picked it up.

'Hello?'

It was Demetrious again.

'Mrs Theakis? Mr Theakis has suggested you lunch with him in his apartment here. Would that be convenient for you?'

Mentally, Vicky punched the air.

'What a lovely idea,' she trilled. 'I'll be there as soon as I can. We're at—'

She cast her eyes around and told Demetrious what street they were on.

It took a little while still to reach the headquarters of Theakis Corp. As the car drew up, Vicky felt the lick of memory. She hadn't been here very often during her marriage, and she only recalled being in Theo's private apartment at the top of the building a couple of times. But it was still strange—unnerving, even—to walk into the building.

Just being in Athens again was strange. Unnerving.

She pressed her lips together. Their marriage of convenience had been working out fine—why, *why* had Theo had to go and ruin everything? Why?

His ego. That was all. His overweening sexual ego that had decided that he might as well have her panting for him, as well…

Memory drenched through her. Not of the time of her brief, wretched marriage, but of last night. And the night before, and the night before that.

She could feel her body react in hot, humid recollection of what it had done a few hours ago, in the darkened tumult of her inflamed desire…

Her nipples were hardening, the pulse at the vee of her legs quickening.

No! God, no! Stop it—just stop it!

With monumental effort she slammed down on her reaction. That wasn't what she must feel! That was fatal—fatal. Even with her cold, light-of-day reasoning about exactly why she had gone along with Theo's outrageous demand that she come to his bed, it was fatal to let her mind go back to what she had done.

Never again. That was what she had to remember. Never again would Theo touch her. Never again would his body move over hers. Never again.

I'm safe now—safe from him. That's all I have to remember. There is nothing more he can do to me. Because I have everything I want from him. Everything.

Except one thing.

She took a breath—a deep one,

What she wanted now from Theo was not something she had to fear. Only be grimly, blackly satisfied by.

I want my own back. I want my own back for what he did to me. And I know exactly how I'm going to get that.

She lifted her chin, picked up her new handbag, and got out of the car.

If it was disturbing to be back in Athens again it was even more disturbing walking into Theo's HQ. This time around, unlike in London, she was shown up to his office straight away, and as she entered Theo's executive suite Demetrious came forward to greet her. If he wondered what she was doing there, why she was suddenly dressed not in chainstore clothes but indeed as 'the former Mrs Theo Theakis', nothing showed in his professionally blank face as he ushered her into Theo's inner sanctum.

Only then, just as she walked in and heard the double doors click shut behind her, did a sense of *déjà-vu* suddenly hit her. This was exactly what she'd done the day that her uncle had announced his bolt-from-the-blue idea—that a man she scarcely knew, but who'd had such a disturbing effect on her right from the very first time she'd laid eyes on him, had asked for her hand in marriage.

She had marched in here, demanding an explanation for so ludicrous a proposition.

Her eyes went to the man now unfolding his tall, lean frame, the same way he had that fatal day.

How on earth had he persuaded her to marry him?

Why the hell did I agree? There must have been another way for Aristides to accept Theo's investment! It was just ludi-crous—ludicrous to go along with what I did!

But she had, and that was all there was to it.

You made your bed...

The echo of the familiar proverb stung in her head, and with an awful hollowing of her stomach she heard not the metaphorical meaning but the literal one.

Bed. Sex. Theo.

That had been what had gone so hideously wrong in their brief, disastrous marriage. And it had been entirely and totally Theo's fault.

If he'd just bloody left me alone...

But he hadn't. And so, without the shadow of doubt, without the slightest sliver of any other possibility, this whole ugly, vile business was *his* fault.

The emotion she had felt building up in her since he had dropped the cheque for *her* money beside her naked body slashed through her again. Powerful, unstoppable—and now roiling in her like a black tide.

Her chin went up. Theo was on his feet.

His face was tight and taut. His eyes dark with cold, icy anger.

'What the hell do you think you're playing at?'

His voice cut at her like a knife.

For a moment, just a moment, Vicky felt a new emotion go through her. She buckled under it, reeling from the vicious hostility in his voice. Memory came at her again, with sickening vividness. This was how Theo had spoken to her on that hideous, hideous day when she had arrived back at his mansion from Jem's and he'd tossed the paparazzo's revealing, condemning photos of her and Jem down on the table in front of her shocked, appalled face.

She felt her throat spasm. *Why does he have to be so angry with me? Why?*

Her throat tightened. There was almost pain in it.

But what was the point of pain? Pain just made her weak, defenceless. She had stood there while Theo carved her into shreds that awful day. Her stammering attempts to justify her actions had been scathingly demolished even before she could get them out. Theo had not listened—had only attacked. Savagely, ruthlessly, totally.

Then thrown her out.

Thrown her out and taken his petty revenge by refusing to hand her over the money she had been promised.

And then—her stomach hollowed—then he had taken a revenge that had not been petty at all...

She felt her spine stiffen. When Theo had thrown his outrageous demand at her in London, her only thought had been how she could protect herself from his vengeance.

But he had not let her do so. He had imposed on her exactly what he had planned all along—her humiliation, at his skilled and expert hands. Allowing her no quarter—no hiding place.

Her eyes hardened.

Well, now it's my turn. My turn for a little revenge. And I will really, really enjoy sticking the knife in you this time around...to give you back what you paid out to me, night after night...

This is just a fraction of what you did to me!

She walked forward. Strolled forward. Her high-heeled sandals moved her hips, the fine material of her dress eased over her body. Her freshly washed and styled hair lifted from her shoulders. Her outfit might have taken an uncomfortably large bite out of her credit card, but she didn't care right now, she just didn't care—she felt and looked exactly the way she wanted.

Elegant. Classy.

A knock-out.

And as she saw the pinpricks of his pupils flare suddenly at her approach she felt confidence flood back into her.

Something else came with the confidence. But that wasn't important. Not now.

She raised an eyebrow quizzically.

'What am I playing at? Why, Theo, I'm here at your invitation. You've invited me for lunch, remember? Upstairs in your penthouse.'

His eyes were masked. Out of nowhere, all the emotion in his face vanished. It was like a smooth, unreadable surface. She knew that face, was very familiar with it. It was a face to be extremely wary of. Well, she was wary, all right. But that wasn't going to stop her. Wasn't going to intimidate her. Not this time. She was, after all, in possession of information that Theo would find it bitter to swallow. But he was going to swallow it all the same. And there was nothing he was going to be able to do about it.

So she just went on standing there, her expression as bland and as smooth as his.

He walked around the edge of his desk. Her eyes stayed fixed on him. For a tall man he was very graceful as he walked. The grace of a tiger approaching its prey.

Instinctively she tensed, then forced herself to let her muscles relax. She wasn't Theo's prey. Not any more.

Never, ever again.

She stood her ground. She would do this. She would do this and win. For once, in their final encounter, she would win.

'Well, in which case, let's head upstairs. I'm sure Demetrious has sorted out lunch for us. Shall we?'

He ushered her from the office, past his PA, and across the lobby to his private lift. As the doors sliced shut on them Vicky felt a burst of claustrophobia. She was not fearful of lifts—but the enclosed space made Theo seem closer to her than she ever wanted him to be again.

When the doors opened directly into his penthouse apartment she stepped out hurriedly. Too hurriedly? Was she betraying her reluctance at being so close to Theo? Well, tough—and too late. She walked forward with the same deliberate, confident air with which she had walked into his office one floor below, and made a beeline for the windows on the far side of the room. She could see the outline of the Parthenon on its rocky hill, the Acropolis, guardian of Athens for time immemorial. She ought to take another visit before she left for London. It was a good time of year to be in Athens—so much cooler than it had been that long, hot summer of her marriage. She could stay a few days in a hotel and see the sights again. No one would know who she was, and she would not come here again, she knew.

Sadness plucked at her. Then a harder emotion. That was yet another crime to be laid at Theo's door. Not just what he had done to her, and to her relationship with her last paternal blood relative, but the fact that he had parted her from her own Greek heritage.

She turned back, so that she could no longer see the outline of the city she loved.

'Would you like a drink?'

Theo was crossing to the drinks cabinet against the wall. Through the double doors that gave on to the dining room Vicky could see a team of staff, busily setting the table, despatched to do so from the executive kitchen on the floor below. It was not the first time she had lunched here. There had been several times when he had had business acquaintances for lunch who had brought their wives, necessitating her presence, as well, to make polite small talk while the men talked business.

Did he bring his women here? The thought stung in her mind before she could stop it. It would be convenient, after all, and the lift descended straight to the car park, so 'guests' could arrive and leave without having to go through the office levels.

Her eyes flickered around. The décor couldn't have been more different from that 'love-nest' on the coast! It was stark and masculine, functional and minimalist. Any women he brought here would have to accept that this was the space of someone who was not prepared to make concessions to their feminine sensibilities.

Well, right now, 'feminine sensibilities' were something she was going to be decidedly short on. This was hardball time. Plain and simple. She wanted to hit at Theo. Hit him in the only spot that was vulnerable.

His ego.

Not that he looked in the slightest bit vulnerable right now. As ever, that aura of power sat on him as seamlessly as his superb hand-tailored suit. As her eyes rested on him, a sense of protest stabbed at Vicky. It wasn't fair—it just wasn't fair! He looked *so* damn compelling that even now, steeled as she was, she could feel the familiar deadly weakness start up inside her just by looking at him.

Let alone remembering…

'Mineral water, thank you,' she said crisply, cutting like a necessary blade through her own treacherous thoughts.

'Still or sparkling?'

The smooth dark tones mocked her, she knew. But she would mirror his cool if it killed her.

'Still will be fine.'

Anything would be fine—anything without alcohol. She needed control—perfect control.

He poured out her drink, adding ice, and handed it to her without expression. Yet there was something moving behind his mask, she knew. Well, she didn't care. He could think what he liked. It was nothing to do with her—not any more.

She lifted her glass.

'*Yassoo,*' she intoned.

He did not respond, merely lifting his own highball to his mouth and taking a slow, considering sip. His eyes did not leave hers.

Something ran between them. Unspoken. Like a line of wildfire in tinder dry grass.

The world stopped around her. Just stopped.

She heard a silent cry in her head. Fear. Absolute fear.

More than fear…

Worse than fear…

'Lunch is served.' The sonorous tones from the doorway to the dining room made the world start again. As her fingers closed more tightly around the chilled column of her glass, she walked into the room beyond. Going through the required rituals of taking her place at the table gave her the chance to regain control of herself.

'I only ever have a light lunch,' Theo said, indicating the array of salads on the table. 'But of course if you would like something more substantial, you have only to say.'

She gave a curt nod of her head. One of the staff was setting out a coffee tray, with a jug of coffee keeping warm on a hotplate. A quick word in Greek to their employer, asking if anything else was required, a brief negative from Theo, and they took their leave. She was left alone with Theo.

She started to reach for the salad bowls, making a selection. She was not hungry. Her stomach was a tight knot. She watched covertly as Theo did likewise, his movements as smooth and economical as always. It came to her that this would be the last time she would set eyes on him…

The world seemed to still again, and then stop completely.

She forced it to keep going again.

Focus—that's all. Just focus.

Theo lifted his fork to his mouth. 'What's this farce all about, Vicky?' he asked.

His voice was off-hand, indifferent. She felt her back go up. Deliberately she delayed in answering him, making a play of taking a mouthful of salad and eating it.

'Well?' There was more curtness in his voice as he prompted her. He did not like to be kept waiting for answers when he wanted them.

Even more deliberately she took a drink from her water glass, forked up some more food.

'I wanted to thank you for the money, Theo,' she answered, her voice bland.

His eyes narrowed infinitesimally. Then, gliding in with a knife thrust she did not see coming, he said, 'It was my pleasure. My very considerable pleasure. Yours, too, of course.'

His eyes unveiled as he spoke, touching her like a caress. A slow, sensual caress. She felt colour flare in her cheeks.

Bastard! He was doing it deliberately. *Don't react—do not react to him!*

She blanked him. It was hard, excruciatingly hard, but she did it.

'I've paid the cheque into my bank already. I stopped off on the way here. I've kept my personal account going—the one I opened before we married—which of course makes it easier for paying in a euro cheque. I dare say I'll suffer from the exchange rate when it's transferred to my London bank, but, given the size of the sum, that won't be too much of a loss.'

She took some more food and continued, her voice with the same light, bland tone. 'Mind you, it will need to stretch quite a long way. The house that Jem's inherited needs a lot of work doing to it to make it habitable again. But it's a wonderful opportunity, of course, and we're both so very excited. A complete new start for us both! We'll be moving there in the summer, which will be lovely. Did I mention the house is in Devonshire? Very near the coast? It's an old house—Victorian, I believe. Rather appropriate, given my name, don't you think?'

She gave a little tinkle of laughter and drank some more water. Her throat was dry with tension. 'We're going to have to do huge amounts to the house, of course. Roof, new electrics—all that boring sort of stuff. That's before we get on to the fun bits like decorating. Still, it will keep us busy! And together, which is even nicer. I always miss Jem when he's not around—we go back *such* a long way, and we stick together through everything. Thick and thin.'

Her eyes were like diamonds. Sparkling and hard. But her gaze as she looked along the table at Theo was limpid, like clear, transparent water. She was hiding nothing from him— every word was the truth. Nothing but the truth.

Theo had stilled. Not a muscle moved in his body. His face was a mask. Then, lifting his highball to his mouth and lowering it again, the movement completely controlled, he spoke. His voice was casual, so very casual.

'You're a fortunate woman. Not every woman can boast a lover who's happy to whore her out for cash.'

His eyes were blank. Expressionless.

'Or aren't you going to tell him how you got the money— by having sex with me?'

She pushed back from the table. Her chair scraped on the tiled floor. As she stood up, she had to cling on to the table to keep upright.

'Will it just be our little secret? Is that it?' he continued, his eyes still with that same strange, expressionless look in them. 'So many secrets to keep, though. The way you like me to stroke your breasts, the way your body ripens for me, the way you give that cry in your throat when you orgasm, the way—'

'You *bastard*!'

Her voice was shrill, ripped from her lungs.

His eyes still looked at her, but now there was a dark, black glitter to them. 'The way you cry out my name as you climax. Will you tell him that, I wonder? Or will that just be another little secret from him?'

'*Shut up!* Shut *up*! You unspeakable *bastard*!

He didn't even register her outburst. His voice was as smooth, as unperturbed as ever.

'No? Not planning on going into that much detail? Not even planning on saying how you whored yourself to me for it?'

Her hand crashed down on to the surface of the table, shaking the crockery violently. Pain shot up her arm, but it was nothing, *nothing*, to the tempest inside her.

'It was *my* money! Mine! You had no right to keep it! No right to it! No right to make me do what you did! I don't have to feel bad about it! It's you, *you* who should feel guilty. You who—'

He was on his feet. His face was a snarl.

'You shameless little bitch! You committed adultery—without the slightest ounce of shame or remorse or guilt!'

She stepped back. Her heart was pounding, pounding with fury and outrage.

'Oh, that's rich—that's rich.' Her voice was hollow. She had started to tremble, the way she had when he had eviscerated her that first, hideous time. '*I* committed adultery? God Almighty, every damn day I was here I had women falling over themselves to tell me they'd had affairs with you—'

'Past tense! I never touched another woman while you were here!'

Her mouth opened, then closed. Then, simply staring at him, she spoke.

'Why the hell not?'

For a timeless moment there was silence. A silence you could cut with a knife. The snarl left his face.

'Why not?' he echoed. 'Because—' he bit out each word
'—I was married.'

Her brows drew together. She stared at him uncomprehend-
ingly.

'It wasn't a real marriage. It was fake from beginning to end.
A total sham.' She took a deep, shuddering breath. 'Are you
telling me you never…you never carried on with *any* of your
women? But you *must* have! It's ludicrous to think otherwise!'

He was staring at her. 'You really thought that?'

'Of course I did! We weren't *really* married! It was for show,
that was all! Of *course* someone like you would have gone on
having sex!'

His mouth tightened. 'Unlike you, I am not in the market
for adultery.' His voice was as cold as ice.

Something snapped inside her. 'It wasn't a question of
adultery! Adultery doesn't come into it!'

'Spare me your moral take on things,' he shot back contemp-
tuously. 'And don't think to worm your way out by using the
basis of our marriage to exonerate your behaviour!' His voice
chilled even more. 'Let alone by trying to make out you were
no worse than me! You committed adultery. I did not.'

Shock was ricocheting round her. Theo had not continued
with his affairs while they were married. It was impossible to
believe, and yet—

*No wonder he seduced me! He had no intention of remain-
ing celibate…*

He had used her. Deliberately and callously. Used her for
sexual relief…

She felt an anger that surpassed anything that she had felt
for him till now. Even when he had thrown at her what he had.

'You absolute bastard,' she said slowly.

Something flashed in his eyes. 'For calling you what you

are? Shameless, conscienceless, without remorse or regret! Bringing shame down on your uncle for—'

Anger leapt in her again.

'*You* were responsible for that! There was no need—no need at all—to tell him why our marriage had ended!'

His face darkened. 'I did my best to avoid telling him. Unlike you.' His voice was scathing. 'I wanted to spare his feelings. But he persisted, insisted on knowing why you had returned to England, why our marriage was being dissolved, and in the end I had to tell him the truth. That there had been someone else, another man.' His eyes lasered into her. 'Perhaps in London, in sophisticated, liberated circles, adultery means little. Here, there is a different attitude. Your behaviour hurt your uncle very much—something that still completely fails to prick your conscience.'

'My conscience is clear!' Her retort was instant, vehement.

'How convenient. How very convenient. You go from my bed to his in the space of mere hours! *Hours!* From sex with me to sex with him before the sun has set!' His voice whipped her, lifting the flesh from her bones. Remorselessly he ploughed on, each word another crack of his cruel whip. 'Then, when you get greedy for the money which you think—you *really* think!— you're entitled to, you come crawling back to me! You sell your body back to me for cash. And you come here to tell me you are giving it to your oh-so-accommodating lover, seeing no need to tell him how you managed to get it. What a very convenient conscience you have, to be sure. But just how convenient, I wonder?'

He had started to walk towards her, down the length of the table. His voice as he spoke was smooth, but it caught at her like fine barbs. In all the hideous maelstrom of emotions inside her she could feel, quite suddenly, her heart rate start to quicken, adrenaline start to run. Fear licked through her. He was still approaching her. She started to back away. It was essential, quite essential, to back away—

His eyes were holding hers, dark and glittering. She felt her stomach hollow.

'How, I wonder, how far will that wonderfully flexible, elastic conscience of yours stretch?'

He was getting closer. She backed away, backed against the wall. He went on coming towards her.

'Stay away from me!' Her voice was high-pitched, adrenaline streaming in her blood, fear—it must be fear!—jumping in her veins.

He did not stop. His eyes still held hers, immobilising her. His voice was smooth, as smooth as the devil's.

'Stay away from you? But that isn't what you want, is it, Vicky? You don't want that at all. *This* is what you want. You wanted it every night this last week—over and over and over again. You couldn't get enough of it...'

He reached his hand out to her. Smoothed down the silken fall of her hair. A shiver went through her, trembling in her body. His hand cupped her face, his thumb stroking along her cheekbone. She felt it in every part of her body.

No! No—don't let him! Don't let him!

She wanted to move—run, hide. But she could not. She could only stand, paralysed, immobilised, the hard, unyielding surface of the wall behind her. The hard, unyielding figure in front of her.

'This is what you want,' he said again, and his other hand slid around the nape of her neck, his fingers slowly moving, sensuously, seductively, on the sensitive skin. She felt weak, boneless.

His eyes caressed her.

'You want this, and you know can have it—don't you? You don't even need to tell yourself it's to get the money you want. And you won't have to tell your lover because of that convenient conscience of yours—the one that allows you to do this...'

His mouth lowered to hers. It moved on hers slowly, languor-
ously, devastatingly. She felt her legs give, and in the same
moment his fingers at her nape strengthened, holding her head
as he took her mouth, opening it to his.

It was bliss. It was heaven. She could not stop, could not
resist, could not do anything except give herself to the sensation firing through her.

He lifted his mouth from hers. The dark glitter in his eyes
shot through her like sparks of fire. Igniting her.

'Still more? Allow me to oblige you—'

He scooped her up. Her body was boneless, clinging. She
didn't care. Could not care. Could not do anything except lift
her mouth to his as he lowered it again, striding through the
room into the lounge. He didn't bother with the bedroom, or a
bed. Even as he lowered her to the sofa he was stripping off his
jacket, tie, shirt. Swiftly, ruthlessly discarding what was unnecessary for the moment. Then he turned his attentions to her.
Her zip was gone in an instant, her dress discarded. Blood
pounded in her veins, hunger in her eyes, her mouth. Oh, dear
God, she wanted him. Wanted the hard, lean length of him on
her, in her. Arousal consumed her like a fire in the undergrowth.

This was no slow coupling. Urgency burned through her, as if
she knew, somewhere dim and dangerous to her, that what she was
doing was madness, folly, a crime so stupid that it would never be
forgiven.. But she could not stop. As his mouth suckled her, pulling
strongly on the rigid, sensitised peaks of her breasts, she held his
head to her, her thighs straining against his. He was hard against
her, so hard, and she felt a leap of raw, primitive excitement lunge
through her. She writhed against him, hungry and urgent. Wanting
him. Wanting him now, right now. His possession, his body in hers,
now, right now. She lifted her hips to him, her free hand straining
down over his naked back. He was still half clothed, but she didn't
care. Wanted only what he was withholding from her…

Her hand slid beneath his waistband, and then her other hand was there, too, unfastening him, freeing him…strong in her hands, powerful and potent, so potent. She gave a rasp in her throat, lifting her hips to him as his tongue laced around her nipples, shooting peaks of pleasure through her that she thought she must die from. But it was not enough, not enough. She had to have more…she had to have all…

'Theo—now, *now*!'

Her voice was urgent, desperate. His head lifted from her, eyes still burning like lasers into hers.

'Theo!' she gasped again, and parted for him.

He drove into her, and she gave a great gasp of pleasure as he filled her. Sensation exploded through her, driving on and on, fire was raging in her. Her hands slid around his back, gripping him to her.

His mouth swooped on hers, devouring her, and she gave him like for like, as urgent as he, more urgent still. He drove into her again, and then again, and each time the sensation that exploded in her was like a hammer of pleasure. With every thrust the ultra-sensitive zone within her sent more and yet more excitement through her. More and more, over and over, and over again, thrust after thrust…

'Theo!'

Her voice was a cry, a gasp of incredulity, as a pleasure so intense that she felt it like a white burning heat flashed out from where it had ignited and sheeted through her body, burning down every fibre of her being.

'Oh, God, *Theo*!'

She gasped for air, for oxygen, but it only fed the flame, sending yet another wave of even deeper intensity and pleasure through her. Every muscle in her body had tautened, and the extreme tension seemed to amplify what was happening to her. She cried out yet again.

Then he was surging in her. She could feel him, filling her, engorging her, convulsing into her. His hands were pressing down on her shoulders, his torso rearing over her, his head lowered from his powerful, straining shoulders.

She clung to him. Clung like a swimmer in a drowning sea, clung to the hard strength of the body over her, clung to him while his body convulsed into hers, and while hers, every nerve inflamed, strained against him.

The moment went on and on and on.

And then, at the limits of exhaustion, it died away.

Leaving her on the shore of the realisation of what she had done.

His weight came down on her, muscles slackening. His head was at her shoulder, and she could feel the heat of his racing breath on her dampened skin. Her exhaustion was total, as if she'd run a mile. Her heart beat in hard, heavy slugs, her pulse, too.

She could feel his face against her. Feel his skin cooling, feel the sleek sweat of desire spent draw the heat from her body. Leaving her cold, so very cold…

His head lifted from her. His eyes looked down into hers. For one moment there was something in them, then it was gone. Quite gone. Now there was only that dark glitter in them again. With long fingers he smoothed the hair back from her sweated brow, a touch that made her shudder deep, deep within, and gazed into her distended eyes.

'Will you tell him about this, your hapless lover? Tell him how you cried out for me as I took you? Tell him how this time—' his voice changed, cutting like a knife into her '—you did not even do it for the money…'

He levered up from her. Standing there, adjusting his clothing. Picking up his shirt from where it hung half off the arm of the sofa, where it had caught, and shrugging himself into it.

Then he walked towards the phone on the sideboard and lifted it.

His Greek was too quick for her, but when he hung up and turned back to her she did not need to understand.

'The car will be waiting for you in the basement. Your flight will be rearranged for when you reach the airport.' His eyes flickered at him. 'I suggest you use the bathroom in the guest room to repair your appearance. You'll forgive me if I make my farewell now.' He walked towards her, lifting her supine, naked body upright. She sagged, unable to support herself, and his arms held her, his fingers around her flanks, indenting into her ribcage. He looked down into her face a moment. Her hair was tousled wantonly over her bare shoulders, her eyes were wide, distended, her mouth bee-stung from his arousal of her.

His eyes had that strange blankness in them; his face was a mask.

'So beautiful on the outside,' he said. 'So deceptive.'

He let her go and walked away, heading, she dimly remembered, for the master bedroom, and presumably its bathroom.

Like a zombie she picked up her clothes. Like a zombie she found the guest bedroom and its en suite bathroom. Some time later, when she was sure the apartment was empty again, she took the lift down to the basement and got into the waiting car. She was driven to the airport where a first-class ticket back to London had been arranged for her.

She wanted to die.

Two days later, when she phoned her British bank to ensure the money had been transferred from her Greek account, she was informed that the cheque had been stopped by its issuer.

Theo had taken his revenge on her yet again.

CHAPTER TEN

THINGS were not going well for Theo. His business affairs were thriving, as ever. His investment in Aristides Fournatos's company was returning handsome profits, and he and the old man had formed a consortium to turn the tables on the company that had tried to buy him out. They were very close to acquisition, but Theo was adamant that the directors of the company should not personally profit financially from any takeover bid. He did not like to see the undeserving reap rewards from their misdeeds—whether they were unscrupulous corporate asset-strippers or an adulterous wife.

But he must not think of that. Must not think beyond the fact that he was now finished with her. Absolutely. Permanently. Stopping the cheque had been the last action he had taken to dispose of her once and for all.

It had been, he now knew, a mistake to do what he had. He had thrown her from him two years ago, and he should have left it at that. He had known this, but for some insane reason he had been unable to stop himself when she had accosted him in London.

Bad mistake. A very bad mistake.

But then his whole disastrous marriage had been a mistake. No, that was not to be thought of. Not to be referred to. It was to be put aside, ignored. It was bad enough that he had to live in the same city as Aristides Fournatos, bad enough that he had to look the man in the eye every day and know that he knew the shocking truth about his niece. And that had been another mistake—telling Aristides why their marriage had ended. He should have stonewalled him, refused to explain. But Aristides had been set on trying to patch things up between them, on visiting Vicky, getting her to come back to Athens. Then Theo would have had to see her again...

And yet he *had* seen her again, and of his own volition He had succumbed to that unforgivable lapse of judgement after seeing her in his office, outraged at being ignored, fire and ice flashing in her eyes.

Mistake. Bad mistake.

And worse to follow.

Offering her that devil's deal, so that he could take his revenge for what she'd done to him two years ago. It had been easy to lure her with the promise of the money she was so greedy for. So self-righteously convinced she was entitled to. Adulteress though she was...

Her words of self-exoneration bleated in his memory—*'It wasn't a real marriage...'*

He slammed his mind shut. But not before one final memory had blazed inside his head.

The last, shaming time he had taken her—the ultimate indulgence.

Ohi! No!

His fingers curved around the pencil in his hand and snapped it like a toothpick. He tossed it aside and reached for another, continuing with his rapid scanning of a printout of latest sales figures. Sales were up, profits were up. His business affairs were thriving.

But he, Theo, was not doing well.

* * *

'More coffee?'

'No, thanks, I'm fine. I'd better make a move anyway.'

Jem got to his feet. His lanky frame made Vicky's studio flat seem even smaller than it was. She could have fitted the entire place into the dining room of Theo's Athens penthouse...

But then, that was what being rich did for you. Bought you penthouses and private islands, ski lodges in the mountains—and 'love-nests' on the coast to take your mistresses to.

Mistresses galore for Theo Theakis—except when he was married.

Because then, of course, he'd had a wife to satisfy his sexual needs.

Like a program running in her brain, thoughts formed in her head as they always did, over and over and over again, without pity, without cessation. So what if Theo had not continued with his affairs during their marriage? That only made it worse—much worse.

He used me. Used me for the sex he hypocritically refrained from getting from his usual sources!

Hadn't it been bad enough thinking he'd seduced her simply as an exercise in his own sexual egoism? Now she had to face something even worse.

I could have been anyone! Anyone at all! Any woman would have done—any woman who was his wife. There for the purpose. The purpose of being a vessel for his sexual relief...that's all I was—all my body was.

Just as her body had been nothing more than a means of exacting his revenge on her. Ruthlessly, deliberately using her pathetic weakness, her criminally stupid vulnerability to him, turning it against her, using it as a deadly annihilating weapon against her.

Right to the very, very last.

Cold flushed through her, sickening and shaming.

Even when she'd been yelling her fury and defiance at him he'd still had to do nothing more than walk up to her, touch her, kiss her...

And take her.

She shut her eyes, shame burning through her.

'Vicky—are you all right?'

Her eyes flew open. The concern in Jem's voice making her instantly tense.

'Yes—fine.' She got to her feet. 'Just a bit depressed—which isn't surprising really, is it?'

She tried to keep the edge from her voice, and failed. Like a pressure cooker with the lid tightly screwed down, she could feel the fury and rage boil within her.

'You know,' Jem was saying, 'I still think the best thing to do would simply be to tell him what Pycott Grange is going to be used for. Surely the man can't refuse to release the money then?'

Vicky's face tightened instantly.

'It wouldn't do any good. He'll never hand the money over. Never.'

Her mouth snapped shut like a clam.

Jem gave a heavy, exasperated sigh, and ran his hand through his hair.

'Well, what about my other suggestion, then? Give the story to the press. OK, the guy's in Greece, but even so, surely the tabloids there would snap up a story about some rich tycoon who won't fund a holiday home for deprived kids?'

'No!' A shudder went through her. 'I could never do that. And anyway, it won't work. Look, Jem, *nothing* will work! The man is a total and absolute *bastard*!'

'Well, what about your uncle, then? The money came from him originally. Maybe he'd give you what he agreed, and then get the original amount back from your ex?'

'No!' Her negation came again, more high-pitched this time. 'Jem, stop it—there isn't any way. There just isn't!'

'Maybe your uncle would simply make a charitable donation, then, irrespective of any deal or whatever that was set up when you married—'

'Jem! No! It's impossible. I can't go to my uncle—I can't!'

Jem's face set. 'Vicky, it's your family, I know, and I don't want to interfere. But think about it—your uncle is rich. It's insane to ignore that. We need the money so urgently—we really do. We can do what we can—get some local help, try and raise money here—but it's just so frustrating knowing that you're owed that money and your ex is too bloody tight-fisted to hand it over.'

Vicky's hands clutched together. 'I'm sorry, Jem. I'm really, really sorry. But I can't get in touch again—I just can't. Please don't ask me to.'

She kept her voice calm, as calm as she could. But Jem's searching eyes looked at her.

'OK, I'll back off.' His arms came around her in a warm, comforting bear hug. 'You're very important to me, Vic, and I don't want you upset by anything or anyone.' He released his hug, but slid big hands either side of her face. Then he dropped a kiss on her forehead. 'You take care now, OK? Promise me?'

He smiled reassuringly at her. 'We'll work something out. Don't you worry. We haven't got this far just to give in now. Look, I tell you what—I'll drive down to Devon tomorrow, see what the latest state of play is down there. Maybe there are areas the builders can suggest we do a temporary, cheaper job on, just for the moment, so we can still open this summer. There are ways and means—there always are.'

He dropped a last kiss on her forehead and let go of her. But even as he released her her arms wrapped around his waist, and she pressed her cheek against his chest.

'Oh, Jem, I'm so sorry—I really am.'

He patted her back. 'That's OK, Vic—truly. I know that whole marriage scene was a bad time. But you've got me—you know that. We go back a long way, you and I. Thick and thin.'

She pulled away from him, smiling up at him.

'Right back to when you thumped Peter Richards from the year above, for lobbing that conker at me!'

'Yeah, and then he thumped me back. I can still remember the nosebleed.' He gave a rueful laugh. 'Well, I always was fool-hardy. Weighing in to fight the big, bad guys.' He glanced at his watch. 'I'd better go. The tube will be shutting down soon.'

'You can stay the night if you want.'

He shook his head. 'No, I'll make a dawn getaway tomorrow morning. Be in Devon by mid-morning.'

She saw him to the door. Her smile was strained by then, but she kept it pinned to her face.

Only when he had gone did it crumple into little pieces.

Theo eased his dinner jacket over his shoulders. He was due at the opera within the hour, and he still had some phone calls to put in to the States. Not that he was eager to get to the opera, either. Or, indeed, to escort Christina Poussos there. But it was a gala of some kind, and she wanted to show off—and show him off, too, at her side.

His face tightened as he checked his dress tie and slid his wallet into his tuxedo. He'd take her back to her own apartment afterwards. He had no intention of bringing her back here, either, to the Theakis mansion, or to his office penthouse.

Above all, not there.

He hadn't used it much recently. It was a damn nuisance that it was part of the Theakis HQ or he'd have sold it straight away. He must buy another city apartment. It might not be as conven-ient as the one at his HQ, but it would have fewer....associations.

It was irritating that he could not dispose of this mansion, either. But it had been the Theakis family residence for too long for him to sell. Even so, he was spending less and less time there.

He'd already sold another property he possessed. One with a sea view.

And far, far too many memories…

He picked up his mobile and headed downstairs. Christina wanted him to arrive early, to collect her from her apartment, but he did not intend to do so. She would want sex, and he was not intending to oblige her. He was not in the mood for sex.

These days he was seldom in the mood for sex.

And when he was it was definitely not Christina that he wanted.

Or any other suitable woman.

He stalked across the wide hallway and into his study, shutting the door with unnecessary force. Then he started to make his calls.

He needed something to divert him. His mood was not good. *Damn her—damn her to hell…*

Anger stabbed through him. She was nothing but a shameless, adulterous—

He cut the thought out of his head. He knew what she was—so what was the point of repeating it? She was out of his life now, and no power on earth could let her intrude again. She had been a mistake—a bad mistake. But that was hardly a reason for making a bad situation worse.

Deliberately, he conjured an image of Christina Poussos to his mind. She was chic, beautiful, desirable. Better still, she quite obviously wanted to restart their former affair—the one that had been interrupted when she'd decided to marry. But now she was back in circulation, her marriage over, and she was eager to show the world that she was still capable of picking the lovers she wanted. Well, maybe he would change his mind and oblige her after all. She had meant little to him the first time around, and she would mean less this time, but her advantage was that she was a known commodity. With Christina Poussos he knew exactly what he was getting.

Unlike—

He cut out again. Like a circuit breaker. A safety trip.

The ring tones on his phone ceased, and the voice of the person he was calling answered. He leant back in his chair and started to talk business.

Another safety trip. He needed a lot of them these days.

It was some twenty minutes later that the house phone went. It would be his chauffeur, reminding him they must set off or miss the start of the opera. That wouldn't bother him, but it would put Christina in a sulk—she liked making a grand entrance. And since he wanted sex from her tonight he didn't want to have to dispose of female sulks beforehand. Not that Christina would deny him her bed. She would be too triumphant to risk taking that tack. She knew all too well that there were any number of women who would follow her. There always had been. He'd always taken it for granted that since he was Theo Theakis he would never be short of willing females to interest him sexually. He was not conceited—merely realistic. It was not a big issue.

Nor was it a major concern in his life. His major concern was Theakis Corp, and ensuring that those in his employ kept their jobs. It was all too easy to see how danger could threaten—Aristides Fournatos was demonstration of that. Theo's expression changed. Despite the disaster that his ill-judged marriage had proved, he did not regret it. He had done the right thing, he knew. Business was a close-knit affair, and mutual co-operation was mutually profitable. He had made substantial money from his investment in Fournatos, and honoured his father's memory, as well, standing by one of his close friends.

His eyes hardened. Honour. A strange word. Meaning nothing—and everything.

She should have told me. Told me right from the start that she could not marry me because she was still involved with another man. Aristides might not have approved—might have wanted to know why she was not marrying this man if he meant so much to her as to have an affair with him—but he would not have persisted in his hopes and plans for a dynastic marriage to underpin and justify my investing in Fournatos.

But she had said nothing. Why? She had been vociferous enough on the whole subject of the kind of marriage that was commonplace in his and Aristides' circles. Vociferous and scathing. Yet not a word on the one subject that would have put an instant stop to the whole notion.

About that she had kept completely silent.

Keeping it her little secret...

Her dirty, dishonourable secret.

Not worth disclosing.

Again in his head he heard her indignantly self-justifying outburst. *'It wasn't a real marriage...'*

Did she really think that gave either of them *carte blanche* to ignore its existence? Did she really think that was what he had done? Had she actually thought that he would continue with other women for the duration of their marriage?

I gave her no cause to think that. None! And she knows it!

No, she had just trotted out that convenient disclaimer of all responsibility for her own act of adultery! Trying to make out he was as culpable as she! Just to exonerate her own despicable behaviour.

He felt anger knife through him, as emotion so strong it seemed to white out in his head.

She went to him from me...

From my bed to his...

The violence of his emotion shook him.

The house phone rang again. Insistent. Intrusive. But he needed its interruption. With visible force he wiped his mind. Took back control of himself.

He lifted the phone.

It was not his chauffeur, but the on-duty security guard. A visitor was at the entrance, asking for him.

'He refuses to give his name or state his business, *kyrios*. Should I phone the police? I have him on camera, if you wish to view him.'

The monitor in Theo's office flickered, cutting to the exterior view of the electronically controlled gates to the driveway. A taxi was pulled up, and standing by the intercom, in full view of the security camera trained on him, was the man who was asking for him.

For a second Theo just looked at the image in front of him. Then, slowly, his face drained of expression.

'Show him in,' he instructed.

'Vicky, these figures don't add up to that total.'

Vicky looked up from her work. One of her colleagues was holding a printout of some financial calculations she'd just produced.

'Oh, Lord, sorry. I'll sort it—' She held out her hand for the papers.

Her colleague handed them over. 'So long as the master file is accurate. I've marked where the súms went wonky,' she said with a smile, and headed back to her own desk.

Vicky stared bleakly at the figures in front of her. They were blurring even as she looked. She just couldn't get her head around numbers these days. Or around anything else. She seemed to be moving in a perpetual fog. Everything seemed so very hard to do—even the simplest things, like making a cup of coffee, or getting up in the mornings. Let alone anything that required the slightest brain power.

Depression—that might be the clinical name for it.

She had another name. But it was not one she must ever, ever give voice to.

It was her secret. Her terrible, unspeakable secret. And she could tell no one. No one at all.

Certainly not Jem. He would be so angry—so appalled and horrified.

Thank God he was away at the moment. Last night she'd nearly cracked in front of him, and it had taken more strength than she could bear to use to hold it together until he had gone. But now at least she had a couple of days without him. Not that the knowledge of where he was did anything to cheer her. She glanced at the clock on the wall. Even now he was probably walking around Pycott with the builder, realising just how daunting the task of making it even partially habitable would be without the money they had been expecting.

Despair crushed her. If only she could go to Aristides! He would give her the money, she knew he would—he was kind and generous, and his heart would be moved by what she and Jem were attempting to do. But she could never go to him. Not now Theo had told him just why their marriage had come to its abrupt premature end.

She was trapped—trapped on all sides. There was nowhere she could go, no one she could turn to.

If only she could go to her mother and Geoff! They couldn't help financially, she knew that, but just to see them again—just to get out of here, flee somewhere as far away as Australia! She was good at fleeing...

But sometimes... Her stomach hollowed with cruel self-knowledge. Sometimes when she fled from the unbearable, what happened thereafter was even worse.

Like when she had fled the island…

She pressed her lips together. No, leaving the island had been essential. And Jem had been there for her—a wonderful, life-saving surprise she had clung to. But she still could not tell him what she had done. She could not. Shame flushed through her.

And if she did run away again this time it would be even worse! Her mother would ask questions, want answers. Would want to know how it was that she had done what she had…

No, she was trapped. Trapped here, in the prison of her enforced silence.

I can't tell anyone—I can't tell anyone what I've gone and done…

Numbly, rubbing a hand across her weary forehead, she called up the master file of the report she'd compiled, and slowly and laboriously started to retype the corrections.

They took a long, long time to do.

Around her heart a cold, tight shell of despair was forming.

Theo crossed to the drinks cabinet in the corner of his study. He normally never went near it unless he had a visitor. But the visitor on his way into the house now would not be offered a drink.

With controlled, economic movements he opened a single malt, poured a shot into a glass, and knocked it back. It was doing grave disservice to a fine malt, but he didn't care. Right now he cared about nothing—except the visitor who was about to walk into his house.

Was he mad to let him in? No man would let such a visitor into his domain.

And yet he had.

But then, he had his reasons.

He wanted to look into the man's eyes. See him face to face. Tell him just what he thought of him. He might… He felt his left hand fist. He might just do more than that…

But not in anger. He would remain, as it was imperative to do, in total and absolute control. That was essential.

With total, absolute control, he set back the empty glass and closed the cabinet. Crossed back to his desk. Pulling back his chair, he sat down, and with total, absolute control he waited for the study door to open.

He could hear the visitor arrive. Hear the front door open and two voices speak, but both were inaudible. Then his door opened. The man walked in.

Theo looked at him. Looked at the man whose face he had last seen looking out at him from the photographs that scum of a paparazzo had placed in front of him in this very room, on this very desk, standing back, waiting—waiting for Theo to take his fill of what they meant, to reach for his chequebook. To pay him the money he required to ensure the photos never saw the light of day.

His eyes rested on him. Expressionless and implacable, dark and impenetrable. The other man's eyes were blue, and they were filled, like the rest of his face, with one expression only.

Anger.

Theo leant back. The movement was again controlled. Then he opened his mouth to speak. To enunciate his views on the man who stood on the other side of his desk.

But the other man spoke first, anger sparking electrically from his eyes, his voice vehement.

'You can tell me one thing, Mr Theakis—and one thing only. You can tell me right now, to my face, just what the *hell* you think you're playing at! And what the *hell* makes you think you have the *slightest* business in keeping my sister's money from her?'

With total, absolute control, Theo froze.

CHAPTER ELEVEN

VICKY was washing out a jumper. It was two in the morning, but she didn't care. She couldn't sleep. Not these days. If she went to bed she simply lay awake, staring up the ceiling, listening to the dying sound of traffic outside in the street.

Thinking.

In the dark it was impossible not to think.

Not to feel.

She would lie there, hour after hour, staring upwards, her emotions stripped naked.

As naked as her body had once been.

Thinking about that. Remembering.

So that was why she was standing here at the kitchen sink, in her thin cotton bathrobe, her hands in suds, rhythmically squeezing warm, soapy water through the woollen jumper. On the draining board a soggy pile of washed clothes was accumulating, waiting to be rinsed. On the other side of the sink was a heap of more clothes to wash. She'd set the radio to a classical music station, and it was playing softly from the top of the cooker. It wasn't a very good choice of music right now, however. Strauss's *Four Last Songs*.

The terrible, ravishing, dying elegies wound in and out of her, the voice of the soprano tearing at her with emotion.

But she must not feel emotion. It was forbidden to her. Forbidden absolutely.

So she went on rhythmically squeezing and dipping, squeezing and dipping.

The sound of the key in the lock made her freeze.

Then she jerked around. The kitchen area of the studio flat was separated from the living/sleeping area by a half-wall that was designed as a breakfast bar, with cupboards underneath for compact storage. An archway to the right of it shielded the front door via a tiny coat lobby.

'Jem?'

Her voice was sharp. He was the only person to have a key both to the block of flats and her own studio.

There was no answer, so she hurriedly, panicking, seized an unwashed garment and hastily mopped the suds from her hands with it. Then she seized a kitchen knife from the knife-block by the toaster. She turned around, heart pounding with fear.

Shock and disbelief blasted through her. The knife dropped from her hand, her fingers suddenly nerveless.

Theo stood in the archway.

He tossed the keys onto the breakfast bar.

'Jem lent them to me,' he said.

Faintness washed over her.

'Jem?' Her voice was weak. Uncomprehending.

'He came to see me,' Theo said conversationally. His voice sounded normal, its familiar deep, faintly accented tones no different from what they had always been in the days when he had spoken to her in such a conversational manner.

But his eyes held the dark glitter that had been in them the last time she had seen him.

Her heart started to pound. Not with the panicked fear of a burglar that she had first felt. With a familiar, heavy pounding that she was very, very used to.

Which was impossible. Because what Theo had just said to her was impossible.

'Jem's in Devon,' she said.

'Wrong,' said Theo. 'He's in Athens. He arrived this evening. We had a very interesting conversation. A very…enlightening…one.'

His eyes were holding hers, holding them with the power of that dark glitter. He stood still, very still, paused in the archway. Vicky's eyes went over him. He was wearing evening dress. It seemed an odd thing for him to be wearing in the circumstances.

But then the circumstances were…unbelievable.

She tried to get her head around them, fixing on the thing that was least unbelievable.

'You were in Athens this evening?' She frowned. But he was here, now, in London.

'Then I flew here,' said Theo. 'You see,' he went on, and something altered in his voice, something that slid along her nerves like acid, 'enlightening as my conversation was, earlier on this evening, it failed to answer all the questions arising therefrom. There are so many questions, but they all have one expression.'

He paused. His eyes glittered with that strange, terrifying darkness.

'Why?' he said softly. 'Why?'

He moved suddenly, and Vicky jumped. But he did not approach her. Instead he walked across to the armchair by the window and sat down. He crossed his long legs, resting his hands on the arms of the chair.

'Start talking,' he said. 'And don't,' he instructed, in the same voice that raised hairs on the back of her neck, 'leave anything out.'

The world was splintering around her. Breaking up into tiny shards, each one so sharp it was cutting her to ribbons. Slowly she reached for a tea towel, dried her hands properly. Then she bent to pick up the knife from where it lay on the floor, wiping it with the tea towel and replacing it in the knife-block. Finally she reached to switch off the radio.

'*Can this be death?*' asked the soprano with tearing beauty.

But death came in many guises. This was one of them.

She walked to the breakfast bar. She needed its support. Her legs had jellied. Shock—that was what it was. Shock was having a physical effect on her that was too great to bear.

'Talk, Vicky.'

She opened her mouth, but no words came. Then, with a rasping breath, she said, 'I don't understand. Why did Jem go to Athens?'

There was a flicker in the dark, glittering eyes.

'He wanted what you wanted, Vicky. He wanted your money.' His voice changed. 'He seemed to think that I was with-holding it unreasonably.' The eyes glittered again. 'He was quite aggressive about it. Which was curious, really, because, you see—' the glitter intensified '—I only let him into my house on the grounds that I was going to personally beat him to a pulp…'

He paused. 'It was as well, was it not, therefore, that he spoke first? After all—' his voice was a blade, sliding between her ribs '—what possible cause could I have to beat your *brother* to a pulp?'

'He's my stepbrother.' Her voice was blank. As blank as the inside of her skull. 'My stepfather Geoff's son from his first marriage. We were at primary school together. That's how Geoff met my mother after his divorce—through my friendship with his son.'

Something flashed in Theo's face. A fury so deep that it should have slain her.

'Why? *Why* did you let me think he was your lover?'

She looked at him.

'Because it ended our marriage and I wanted out.'

Her voice was calm, so very calm. What else could she be? The inside of her head was blank—quite, quite blank.

At her answer she saw his hands bite over the arms of the chair. 'A simple "I want a divorce" would have sufficed.' The scorn in his voice gutted her.

She couldn't answer. It was impossible. Impossible to say it. To anyone.

It was her own terrible, shameful secret.

No one could know. No one in the world. Not Jem, or her uncle, or her mother. No one.

She watched Theo's mouth thin into a tight, whipped line. His eyes were like spears touching her skin, ready to indent into the flesh beneath.

'Your brother is unhappy. He feels—besmirched. Slandered.'

'He was never supposed to know. He shouldn't have gone to Athens. He should have gone to Devon, like he said. I told him you wouldn't give me the money. I told him.' Her voice was still calm.

He mirrored it back. 'But you omitted the little detail of why.'

Her eyes flickered. 'It wasn't relevant.'

The tightening of his hands over the arms of the chair came again.

'Nor relevant to your uncle, either, I presume?'

'No.'

'Nor, of course—' his voice was very calm now, his eyes resting on her, the glitter gone, quite expressionless '—to me.'

She gave a little shake of her head.

'No,' she said.

There was silence. Only the sound of traffic in the street below. And the thudding of her heart, beat by beat by beat.

'Yet you wanted, that money very badly,' he said. 'So badly, you made a whore out of yourself.'

She met his eyes. 'No. Whores get paid. The money was not for me. I expect Jem has told you that.'

'Yes. He was quite discursive on the subject. You may be glad to know, if you consider it in the slightest *relevant*, that I have handed him a cheque that will cover the entire restoration and refurbishment costs, plus running costs for five years.'

'That's very good of you.' Her voice was hollow.

'If you had told me what you wanted the money for I would have given it to your stepbrother. And if you had told me he was your stepbrother, not your lover, I would not have thought you an adulterous slut.'

His voice was still conversational. It sliced through her like a surgeon's blade.

'So why did you?' he asked. 'Let me think you an adulterous slut? Because you did so quite deliberately. You had so many opportunities to put me straight…'

The glitter was in his eyes again.

'You didn't take one of them. Why?' The softness of his voice eviscerated her, as once his fury had done.

She had thought his fury unbearable. She had been wrong.

His dark, glittering eyes rested on her across the small space of her studio.

'Vicky, I have flown fifteen hundred miles. It's four in the morning for me. I scrambled my pilot when he was having dinner with his wife. So you *will* give me answers. Believe me, you will give me answers.'

His eyes were slicing through her. Inch by inch.

'Why did you let me think you were a faithless bitch?'

Her fingers were pressing onto the tiled surface of the breakfast bar. Pressing so hard that at any moment, any moment now, they must surely snap.

'I told you—I wanted out of our marriage. And it worked, didn't it?'

'You slandered yourself and your stepbrother, you shamed your uncle. Or wasn't that *relevant*?'

'No.' None of that had been relevant.

'So what *was*, Vicky?'

She couldn't answer. She could never answer. Silence bound her for ever. Bound her to her terrible, shameful secret.

'I've had a long time to think about this, Vicky. If you won't give answers, I will.' He stood up. The movement made her jerk.

He was starting to come towards her. Tall and lean and dark. And terrifying. Her eyes distended. Flaring with terror.

The unfastened jacket of his tuxedo swung, revealing the muscled narrowness of his waist, the whipped leanness of his hips.

She could feel his power. She had always felt it.

And it had always, always terrified her. Time dissolved away and she saw him again, turning to be introduced to her, those dark eyes looking down at her so impassively. She had felt his power then.

She felt it now.

Desperately she clawed her hands over the surface of the breakfast bar.

'Stay back, Theo—'

The words broke from her.

'Answers, Vicky.'

He stood there, on the far side of the bar, a foot away from her. So close. Terrifyingly, terrifyingly close.

'Tell me why you let me think you had a lover. Tell me—'

His voice impelled her. His gaze compelled her.

Terror consumed her. Terror and desperation.

She threw back her head.

'Why do you *think*, Theo? You'd just had sex with me!'

There was scorn in her voice, forcibly injected under an intensity of pressure. Her fingertips were still pressing into the tiles, the veins on the backs of her hands standing out like ropes.

'Sex with the only woman you were going to allow yourself so you didn't have to be celibate while married to Aristides Fournatos's niece! So don't damn well stand there and look for answers—because *that's* the reason! I met Jem at the airport because I picked up a text message on my mobile from him, saying he was Athens. I was so upset over…what had happened on the island…I just had to get away. We went sightseeing and talked about the house he was sent to inherit, how it would be brilliant for a youth centre, only we would need a lot of money to do it up. He asked me if I could line up the funds out of what you'd promised to release to me when our marriage ended. The time away from you had me realise that I had to get away from you—permanently. So when you threw those vile photos in my face I grabbed at the chance to make it the reason for ending our marriage immediately. And it worked, didn't it? *Didn't it?* You couldn't wait to lay into me—to slash me to pieces! And then throw me out like garbage!'

She fell silent, finishing on a harsh, indrawn breath, her eyes spitting at him.

He was standing very still. A nerve was ticking in his cheek.

His voice was controlled. Very controlled. 'When you came to the penthouse you accused me of adultery myself. All through our marriage you assumed I was sleeping with other women. Was that why you let me think you had a lover, too? To get even with me?'

'It was to get *away* from you! What the hell does it matter whether you were carrying on with other women or using me as some kind of bloody sexual relief?'

His eyes were resting on her. 'You're right, it doesn't matter. Because neither is true. But what does matter…' his voice was conversational again, but the nerve was still ticking at his cheek in his stark, expressionless face '...is why you thought either was true—and why that upset you.'

'I wasn't *upset*—I was *angry*! Angry at being used like that!'

'But I didn't use you in that repellent way. Nor did I commit adultery with any other women during our marriage. So now you don't need to be angry any more, do you?'

Her face contorted. 'How the hell can you say that?' she demanded viciously. 'After the way you treated me—forcing me to have sex with you for the money, saying what you said to me!'

He gave a shrug, his eyes never leaving her. 'I behaved like that to you because I thought you had taken a lover, that you still had a lover, and yet were prepared to have sex just to get the money you thought you were entitled to. All you had to do to stop me behaving like that was tell me the truth. But you didn't, did you? You let me go on thinking that about you even when it was no longer necessary. So why, Vicky? Why did you do that?'

He had cut the ground from her feet. She felt herself falling—falling down into the bottomless pit that waited to consume her.

But she mustn't fall. She must fight. Fight with all the weapons she could.

There was only one problem—she had no weapons left. No words. Only a terrible, gaping hollow of horror opening up inside her. She stared at him, wordless, defenceless.

His eyes were moving over her face. The nerve at his cheek had stopped. His voice, when he spoke, had changed.

'Tell me something, Vicky. If I do this now, will you be angry?'

His hand reached to her. Thumb moving across her lips.

'Does that make you angry, Vicky? What about this? Does this make you angry?'

The backs of his fingers drifted over her cheek, then turned to stroke with soft, searching movements over the delicate flesh of her ear, spearing gently, so gently, into her hair.

'What about this, then? Do you feel angry when I do this to you?'

His fingers closed around her nape. Drew, with ineluctable pressure, her face towards him, as with slow, aching descent his mouth moved down to hers.

His kiss was velvet, his lips as soft as silk, his touch as smooth as satin.

He lifted his head away from her.

'Angry, Vicky?' he asked softly, so very, very softly.

Her body was boneless. Her palms collapsed against the cool surface of the tiles. She looked into his eyes. Deep, fathomless. Eyes to drown in.

His face swam before her. On the surface of the breakfast bar a single tear splashed like a diamond.

'Theo, please—don't do this to me. Please.' Her voice was a whisper. 'Please.'

Another tear splashed.

He was looking at her. She could not see him. He was out of focus. Tears were spilling from her eyes.

'Please don't do this to me. Please.'

Greek broke from him. She did not know what it meant, but she heard the shock in his voice. The disbelief.

She knew why. She wanted to die. Fall through the earth into that bottomless pit beneath her, the one that swallowed up all those like her. The fools of the world.

She stared at him through the tears blurring her vision.

'Please go, Theo. Please. Just go. *Just go.*'

She felt her body slacken, felt herself grope for the high stool and heave herself onto it before she collapsed. Her head bowed. Tears were streaming down her cheeks.

'Vicky! *Cristos!* Vicky!'

He had come around the edge of the bar, his arms enfolded her. For one brief, anguished moment she let herself cling to him. Then she drew away. Dragged herself from him.

'Is this answer enough for you, Theo? Is it? *Is it?* Are you happy now? Have you got what you wanted? Just like you got what you wanted from me when you hunted me down? Got me into your bed! And you're right—so bloody, bloody right! What does it matter whether you used me or not? It was all the same to you in the end! Sexual relief or sexual ego! What did it *matter*? What did it matter? It was all the same to you and—oh, God—it didn't make any difference to me! How could it? How *could* it? You made a fool of me either way! A stupid, idiotic fool!'

A laugh broke from her. High and humourless.

'Did you read me wrong, Theo? Did you think I was like all those other women, falling over themselves to tell me they'd had affairs with you, or wanted one, or wanted another one? That I'd just be like them? Enjoy the physical pleasures you had to offer, be chic and sophisticated and blasé about the whole thing like them? Well, I couldn't! And I *knew* I couldn't! I went into that marriage never thinking for a single instant that you'd take that line! I never for a moment dreamt you'd think anything else! Our marriage was a sham, just for show—of *course* you would go on having your normal sex life! When you turned on me I didn't know what to do! I tried to stonewall you—tried so damn, damn hard. But you wouldn't lay off! You kept right on coming. And I tried to stop you—I tried and I tried. And it was the same when you pulled that devil's deal on me! Making me go back to you if I wanted my money for Jem's project! Do you know why I went along with that—do you?'

She glared at him, her face contorted through the tears still running down her cheeks.

'Do you think I did it for the damn money? Well, I didn't!

I wanted the money for Jem, but that wasn't the reason I did what you wanted me to do! I did it to show myself—to show *you*!—that I *could* be just like all those bloody other women! I *could* have totally meaningless sex with you—the only kind you like! The only kind you want! I did it so I could make myself immune to you. To make myself hate you, big-time! And, my God, it should have worked! After everything you did to me, said to me, and that very last nightmare time of all—my *God*, I should have hated you! You were so vile to me, and horrible, and…and…'

She couldn't go on. Couldn't do anything. She had told her terrible, shaming secret, the one she shouldn't tell anyone—anyone at all. And she had told it to the very worst person in the world to tell.

'I should have been immune to you,' she whispered.

But she wasn't. She wasn't immune to him. She would never be. That was the power he had over her, the power that terrified her.

She took a deep, shuddering breath.

Looked at him. Looked right at him.

'Just go, Theo,' she said. Her voice was cracking. She was cracking. Cracking into fragments. 'Just go.'

But he didn't go. He stepped forward to her again, to where she had shrunk from him. He said something to her in Greek. It might have been Greek for idiot—she wasn't sure. Her Greek wasn't very good any more. If so, she wasn't surprised. The word suited her. It was what she was. An idiot. A fool. A moron. One after another the words tolled through her brain, each one breaking her into smaller and smaller fragments. Her tears had stopped now. All run out. She was just a sodden, dripping mess.

Like her life.

She heard him say the word again—the one that probably meant idiot. *Elithios.* That was what it sounded like. Did he have to keep repeating it? She knew she was that—an idiot. Who else but an idiot would have done what she had?

She started to cry again. It seemed to be the only rational response in the circumstances.

Then Theo's arms were coming around her. She was being crushed against him, his arms like steel bands around her. It made her cry more. The tears soaked into his shirt, because there wasn't anywhere else for them to go. He hugged her more tightly, saying more things to her she couldn't understand. Then he slid his arms from her and she nearly toppled off the high stool, but he caught her, held her face between his hands.

'Idiot,' he said, in English this time. His eyes looked into hers. 'I thought myself a clever man—and all the time I was an idiot. Blind to what was right in front of me. Blind to everything—except one thing. One thing.' His gaze searched hers. 'This,' he said.

He kissed her. Warm and close and for such a long, long time. Then his lips left her mouth and kissed her eyes.

'*Matia mou,*' he told her. 'My eyes. My lips. My heart. My wife.'

He kissed her mouth again. This time it was warm, and close, but more—more than that. She felt the flame light in her body.

Then she was being lifted off the stool and carried, still being kissed.

Fear sprang in her.

'Theo! No—please! I can't do this! I can't. *I can't!*'

He crossed the short distance to the bed, its duvet crumpled from where she had thrown it back, sleepless and tormented, an hour ago.

'You can,' he said to her, and lowered her down. 'You must. And so must I.'

He took off his jacket and tossed it aside, and then his dress tie and shirt. Then the rest of his clothes.

Then he came down beside her. 'It's imperative,' he said to her, 'that we do this. Or the idiocy in our blood will take us over for ever. And we must not allow that, either of us. Not any more. Never again.'

He parted her bathrobe, spreading wide the material.

'My most beautiful one,' he said. Then he lowered his head and kissed each breast.

She shut her eyes. There was nothing she could do. Nothing at all. All will was gone. There was nothing left except sensation. Slow and sensuous and sweet. As sweet as honey…the honey that was easing through her veins.

His body was warm to her touch. Warm and strong. He murmured Greek to her, words she did not know, had never known, never heard. But they were honey in her ears, as his touch of her body was honey in her veins.

Slowly he kissed her, slowly he aroused her, slowly he entered her, holding her and cradling her, taking her with him on the journey he was making, to a land he had never visited before. Nor she.

They went to the land together, and found that distant shore, which was so close, so very close, after all. As close as their bodies to each other.

She cried again as the climax consumed itself in her, tears that came from a place deep within her.

'Don't cry,' he said, and held her close. 'Don't cry.'

He soothed her till her tears had ebbed away, easing from her but never letting go of her, folding her to him so that her cheek rested on the strong wall of his chest. Her heart was full within her, but a great grief ran through her still.

She lifted her head to look at him.

Her eyes were troubled. So very troubled.

'Theo—thank you. Thank you for giving me this time now. It's taken away so much of the stain of what happened in

Greece. And I'm grateful, very grateful to you for that. But go now—please. Please go.' She swallowed painfully.

She sat up more, so that she was farther away from him and could half wrap the duvet around her. Then, with another swallow, she began to talk.

'I should never have married you. I knew right from the start that I should not. Not just because I didn't approve of our reasons for doing so—I gave in to the pressure anyway, for my uncle's sake—for another reason. One I refused to face up to until it was far, far too late.' Her eyes gazed down at him, still troubled. 'A marriage like the one we went through could only possibly work if both parties felt the same about it, and about each other. To me it really was a sham, a show, nothing more— a charade meaning absolutely nothing beyond the mere surface. It was nothing more than play-acting, with me cast very temporarily in the role of Mrs Theo Theakis. The play would have finite run and then we'd both go off stage and get on with our real lives again, the purpose of the play achieved. That's why…'

She swallowed yet again, and though she did not want to speak, she did, 'that's why I was so horrified when it actually finally dawned on me that you were…were making a move on me. I kept thinking I must be mistaken—I *had* to be mistaken! I mean, of *course* you couldn't be doing what I thought you were! This wasn't a real marriage—it wasn't anything! The very idea that you would look at me…think of me…in that way was just absurd! And when I finally accepted that in fact you *did* think of me in those terms—it made me angry. It made me so, so angry. How *dared* you do so! Because to me there could only be one possible reason why you were doing it. It was an exercise in power. That was all. Flexing your sexual ego while you continued merrily with the women who'd made it so clear to me that that was your usual practice.'

A painful breath shook through her.

'But I couldn't cope with that—I knew I couldn't. I knew I couldn't treat sex with you the way those other women did. And I knew—oh, God, I knew—that for you I wouldn't be anything more than any other woman was.'

She shut her eyes again, then opened them determinedly. 'Even when you threw at me that you had never slept with any other woman during our marriage, it just made it *worse*! It threw a whole new hideous light on what you'd done to me. You'd played the arch hypocrite—observing the letter of our marriage, refraining from your usual practice—but then, of course, realising you were facing months of celibacy, you'd decided that you might as well recourse to the one woman with whom you could, by your terms, have sex. Me.'

She shook her head slowly. 'Oh, God, that made me even angrier! To be *used* like that! *Used!* Because it meant it didn't matter who the hell I was—anyone you'd married for the reasons you and my uncle thought necessary—anyone would have done!'

'So it didn't matter. Because the outcome would be the same either way. When our marriage came to its allotted end, that would be the end of what you wanted from me. I would go home, as arranged, and that would be that.'

She pulled the duvet more tightly around her, as if it were to stanch a wound.

'That would be that,' she said again, and her voice was bleak. As bleak as winter wind. Then she forced a smile to her mouth. It was a little twisted, a little wry—and very rueful.

'I didn't handle things very well—did I, Theo? I should have been up-front with you. After all, you'd been up-front with me, that time I came to see you after Aristides had done his Victorian novel stuff on me. You were very up-front about why, in fact, a marriage on the terms we made did make sense—was necessary. So, when I finally realised you were making a move on me, I should have been up-front with you, shouldn't I? Simply told you that, unlike your other women, I couldn't handle an affair—as it would have been, in essence—like the one you wanted. And if you really thought our marriage meant you couldn't or shouldn't continue with other women, then I should have told you that you either had a choice of celibacy or dissolving our marriage earlier than we had intended to. Because I just couldn't handle anything else.'

Her smile twisted painfully. 'So in a way it's all been my fault, hasn't it? My fault for not being up-front with you. My fault for being stupid and weak enough to go along with what you wanted of me, and then, worst of all, to panic the way I did and let you totally misinterpret my relationship with Jem so that I could escape from you and know you wouldn't come after me again.'

Her fingers started to pleat the edge of the duvet.

'I just should have been honest with you all along.' Her eyes rested on his face, as impassive as his eyes, which were just looking at her steadily. He had one arm crooked behind his head. Absently, with a slice of pain that seemed to scrape along every raw nerve in her body, she took in the roughened line of his jaw, the feathered sable of his hair, the complex muscula-ture of his shoulder and lifted arm, the strong column of his throat. She would not be seeing them again. She would not be seeing him again. Everything was sorted now—all the truth told. Now it was time for Theo to go. Anger spent, poison lanced, all the secrets and lies disclosed. They could both now get on with their lives.

She would move to Devon with Jem to help run Pycott, visit her mother and Geoff in the autumn, hopefully even make peace with her uncle. But she would not go to Greece again.

That would be too painful, even now. Especially now.

Now there was only one more secret left—one more lie of omission.

That could never be told. Must never be told.

Because there was no point in telling. It would serve no purpose. None at all. So she would keep silent still, the secret deep within her to the end of her days.

'So why did you sleep with me?'

His voice startled her.

He was looking at her, his expression still impassive. 'You say you didn't want an affair with me, as you termed it, and yet you *did* sleep with me when I met you on the island. I'm curious why.'

There wasn't any feeling in his voice, but it was not emotionless in the way that could chill her like freezing water seeping into her shoes. His voice was simply—curious. Enquiring.

She gave a half-shrug. 'I just gave in, that's all. I mean, Theo, after all, it would hardly have come as surprise to you. I'm sure better women than me have given in. You're pretty hard to resist.'

'You managed pretty well.' His riposte was dry.

His eyes rested on her. They were still impassive. But they were veiled—veiled in a way she had not seen before.

'I'll be honest with you—your reaction surprised me. I'd realised how alien the whole concept of a dynastic marriage was to you, and when I realised that was what Aristides wanted as part of our financial arrangement I was very sceptical that it could ever work with someone who had not been brought up to accept such things as normal. Yet I decided in the end that your phlegmatic English temperament would actually make it possible after all. You were capable of being composed and formal, I had noticed that the few times we were together before our marriage, and so I decided to go along with it. However, even within the temporary terms we'd agreed, it was still clearly something you found it hard to get your brain around. Then there was the whole business of adapting to life in Greece, having not been brought up there. You didn't speak the language well, you were feeling your way into being Mrs Theo Theakis, with a life and lifestyle you weren't used to. So I gave you time—it would have been stupid to do otherwise. Besides, I was so busy at work with Aristides's company, as well as keeping my own affairs in order. Time is always the scarcest resource for me, Vicky. I knew from what had happened to your uncle's business that the danger comes when you take your eye off the ball, and that wasn't going to happen to me. So I know I didn't have a great deal of time for you. But I argued that that was all to the good—it gave you the space you needed to make the adjustments you had to make.'

He shifted his weight slightly, his fingers beneath his head flexing at his neck.

'Besides, though you were half-Greek, your nature was English. That was obvious. Obvious not just in your appearance, but in your taste and behaviour. All those understated clothes you wore! Very elegant, very restrained. Just like the way you conducted yourself. You didn't get emotional, you weren't demonstrative, you never picked up on any of the darts thrown at you by the likes of Christina Poussos. And you never picked up on something else, either.'

For a second so brief she thought she must have imagined it, the veil from his eyes lifted. Then, with a sweep of long lashes, it had come down again.

'I have to tell you, appalled as you may be, that it was always my assumption that our marriage would not be a sham in one respect. You said just now that I would have married anyone who was Aristides Fournatos's niece for the reasons I married you, but that isn't actually true. I would never have married a woman I did not find sexually attractive. It would not have been…kind…to her to do so. But you, obviously, were sexually attractive. It would therefore be perfectly possible to have a non-celibate marriage. However, as I've just said, I knew I needed to allow you time to make the adjust-ments necessary to being my wife for the duration we'd agreed on. By then, you will appreciate, I had been celibate for longer than was usual for me. So I was…keen…to remedy that situation.'

It wasn't icy water that was seeping into Vicky as she listened. She had seen Theo arctic with fury, had felt his freezing anger strip the skin from her bones.

But this—this was worse. This was Theo being a man of his class, his wealth, his circle, his normality. Deciding it was time to have sex with a woman he'd always intended to have sex with, whom he would not have entered into such a show marriage with on any other basis other than that she was suffi-ciently sexually attractive to him to warrant it.

He went on speaking. That same light, discursive tone.

'So that is what I set about doing. It was very simple—I merely had to signal to you that the time had come to do what we would both enjoy. I had realised in those initial weeks that I would actually enjoy it more than I had originally assumed. That was because of you, you see. I was finding that your Englishness—all that understated, under-emotional cool—was proving surprisingly alluring. Intriguing. And as I proceeded with "making a move" on you, as you phrase it, it became yet more so. I realised that I was starting to want you really very much. Even if we had not been married, by then I would most definitely have sought an affair with you. Being married to you, in fact, merely added yet another layer of…allure…to you. It presented me with a façade of intimacy, and yet I had not laid a single finger on you. And then, I'm sorry to say, you made the most significant contribution to my condition.'

He looked at her, and somewhere very deep at the back of his eyes she could see something. Something that started, very slowly, to turn her inside out.

'You resisted me. Avoided me. Blanked me. Stonewalled me. Fatal—completely fatal. Were you doing it on purpose? A feminine manoeuvre? I didn't know, and I didn't care. It wasn't relevant anyway. Because there was only one place you were heading for. Only one place I wanted you to be. And I got you there. Of course I did. There was no possibility of anything else. You wanted me as much as I wanted you. So I got you to the island, was there waiting for you, and I took you to my bed.'

There was something strange in his eyes.

'If you had simply stayed there none of this would have happened, you know. We would have done what I had assumed all along we would do. We would have had a mutually en-joyable affair, for the duration of our marriage, and then, when it was no longer necessary for us to be married, we would have parted very amicably and gone our separate ways. That was my intention.'

He stilled. Vicky felt her heart slow. Her fingers clung to the duvet cover as she gazed down at him, half-fearful, half-numb.

'But you didn't stay, did you? You ran. You ran to another man. And in the moments when I looked at those photos of you with him I felt something I had never in my life felt before. Do you know, Vicky, what it was?'

She swallowed. 'Your ego denting.' Her voice was hollow.

He gave a laugh. Harsh and humourless.

'Jealousy. Raw and primitive and leaping in me like a monster. The green-eyed monster, devouring me. I'd never felt it in my life before—why should I have?—and I didn't even realise what it was. I just…possessed it…and it possessed me. Raged through me. It ate me alive from the inside out.'

She could see the cords of his neck standing out, the muscles of his arms tensed like steel.

'Why? *Why* did it do that? What the hell was it, this

jealousy? When Christina was my lover and announced to me that she was marrying I gave her sapphire earrings and my best wishes. When any other lover terminated a relationship before I did, my reaction was the same. The most I felt was irritation if the timing was inconvenient, or if it had been done deliberately to try and get a reaction from me. So where the *hell* did that monster come from when I saw you in those photos?'

She fingered her duvet.

'You're Greek, Theo. It's probably some kind of atavistic response, seeing how I was legally your wife at the time. So it wasn't really jealousy, just a bit more than a dented ego. It was that Greek macho male pride, self-regard, whatever...'

He said a word in Greek. She had a bad feeling she knew what it was, and it was something to do with the male reproductive system of cattle. Or possibly the far end of the bovine digestive system.

Then he spoke again. His voice was different now.

'But there was something else besides the monster eating me alive. Something else that, although it didn't devour me in tearing strips, drained me—quietly, silently, almost unnoticeably—drained me of my lifeblood.'

His right hand, which had been lying inert at his side, lifted. It touched along her knuckles as her fingers clutched the duvet to her. Then he twined his fingers into hers.

'I hurt, Vicky. I hurt so much.'

His voice was quiet.

'I hurt. But it was mortal pain, so I could hardly feel it. Not beneath the monster tearing me to shreds. But it was there all the same, all the time. Invisible, unnoticed, ignored. Until tonight. Until now.'

His fingers tightened on hers. Everything had gone very, very still all around her. Nothing moved. No breath in her lungs. No blood in her veins. All quite, quite still.

He looked up at her. With eyes that were not veiled.

'Why did you run from me that morning on the island? You said you panicked—but why? Why didn't you just turn on me and berate me for what I'd done? Why did you let me tear you to shreds about your adultery? Why did you let me do what I did to you when I made you come back to Greece? You've given me answers, Vicky—but there's one more truth to tell, isn't there? *Isn't there?*'

His grip on her was drawing her down to him. She could not pull back.

'Isn't there, Vicky?' he said again. Insisting—insisting on the truth. *All* the truth. One last secret, one last lie undone.

His hand slid from his neck to hers, holding her with effortless power, so that she could only look down into his face from so, so close.

'I'll answer for you,' he said. His eyes poured into hers. 'You did what I did—and, like me, you never intended to, but it happened all the same. To both of us, Vicky. To *both* of us. And I'm going to say the words to you, so that you can hear them from me and not be afraid—not any more, never again. *S'agape.* I love you. Now say the same, Vicky— say the same. You can do it because I can do it. It's weird and strange and unbelievable—but we must believe it because it is the truth. *S'agape.* Say it, Vicky, *matia mou.* My eyes. My love.'

How hard it was, to say the truth. Even in a whisper.

'*S'agape*, Theo.'

He drew her down to him and kissed her gently. Then he cradled her in his arms and drew the duvet over them both.

'What would you say,' he said, and his breath was warm on her cheek, 'to another wedding?'

She felt love—hers and his—flow between them. A levelling tide that floated them away to the shores of that land they would never leave now, through all that might ever happen, safe in what they had.

She smiled against his mouth.

'I'd say yes,' she said.

EPILOGUE

SUN dazzling on the sea. The scent of thyme, crushed beneath the feet of the wedding guests. The whiteness of the chapel walls against the blue of heaven above.

Vicky stood with Theo, arm in arm in the narrow doorway of the tiny chapel on the hill, on the island, and all around in the clear bright sunlit air was light, pouring down like a blessing on their union.

The guests came forward to embrace them. Her mother and Geoff, hugging her, then her uncle, tears unashamedly in his eyes, and Jem, wrapping her in his bear hug and telling her to avoid the paps in future because he was done with being fool-hardy and rushing off to confront vengeful husbands intent on grievous bodily harm to him.

She laughed, and cried, and laughed and cried again. Her mother was kissing Theo, and Geoff was pumping his hand, and Jem was slapping him on the back, and Aristides was envelop-ing him in the kind of embrace that no Englishman could ever give another man, then turning to her mother and embracing her even more tightly, telling her thickly that his brother was calling down blessings from heaven on his beautiful daughter. Then he was steering them all down the narrow path to the stonewalled villa, which was nowhere near big enough for the party except on the shady terrace, where the wedding break-fast was spread out for them.

The officiating priest, a personal friend of Aristides, had received his brother's daughter into the Orthodox church for her wedding—her real wedding this time, her real marriage. The bride and groom were seated side by side, while her parents and stepbrother and uncle raised their brimming champagne glasses to toast their happiness and their future.

Then a team of staff emerged from the sleek cruiser moored at the tiny quay, and proceeded to present a meal fit for a Michelin starred restaurant.

It was several hours later, and the sun was westering, before the wedding guests started to make their way along the quay to embark upon Theo's cruiser, which would take them back to the mainland. With many embracings, and yet more tears and laughter, they took their leave, and Vicky and Theo watched them go, their arms wound about each other's waists. A final wave, a final blown kiss, then the engine roared and the cruiser cut its wake through the azure waters, heading away.

They watched till it was out of sight.

Then turned to one another.

'So, Mrs Theo Theakis, what do you propose we do now?' asked Theo.

'We could clear the table,' said Vicky.

'Done already. My staff are well trained.'

'Do the washing up?'

'Also done already.'

'Well, there must be something we should do.'

His eyes glinted.

'There's certainly something *I* should do. This.'

His fingers smoothed the fabric of her wedding gown from one shoulder.

'And this,' he said, and his lips smoothed the skin beneath. 'And similarly…'

He performed the same task to her other shoulder.

'Then, of course, there is this.' His hand went to her back, and with a single fluid movement drew down her zip. 'Why, Mrs Theo Theakis, you do not appear to be wearing underwear…'

'It's the heat,' she murmured.

'Ah, well, that is something we can remedy, I believe.' The glint in his eye, the deliberate not touching of her naked back, was sending tiny delicious sparks through her. 'You may find it, Mrs Theo Theakis, cooler indoors. Shall we?'

He guided her inside the villa, into the single bedroom. With the double bed.

'Much cooler,' she murmured.

'Oh, I think we can do better yet,' he said. The jacket of his wedding suit had long ago been discarded, and still hung around the back of the chair he'd sat in for the breakfast. His cuffs were undone and his shirtsleeves rolled up. His tie hung loose around his neck, the top button of his shirt unfastened. Now he proceeded to unbutton the rest of it.

'Allow me to help,' said his wife. 'Wives should always help their husbands in all those little tasks they like help with.'

One by one her fingers slipped his buttons, drawing the fine material apart, slipping it from his broad shoulders. Then, as he stood stock still, no muscle moving, she unbuckled his belt and started on the fastenings of his trousers.

His hands moved like lightning, imprisoning and lifting.

'Some tasks,' he said, and there was a tightness in his voice she'd have been deaf not to hear, 'may prove a little…precipitate…if helped with. Allow me, instead, to reciprocate.'

He drew her loosened dress from her, exposing first one breast and then the other. They were full, engorged already, their tips like coral. He touched each lightly, felt them flower at his touch. Sensation shot through her.

He let her gown fall to the floor. She left it there. She would tidy it later. But now, right now, it was time for one thing only.

She took his hand and lifted it above her breasts, to her heart.

'Roll back time, Theo. Make the past come back again. But make the present now the past. This the reality. Now. For us both. Now and for ever.'

He turned his hand in hers, and took hers with his, raised it to his lips.

'Now and for ever,' he said.

For one long, timeless moment they gazed into each other's eyes, and all the needless pain and torment were undone.

Then he let go her hand and replaced his own at her breast.

'Now,' he said, 'where were we?'

'You were starting to make sensual, passionate, bliss-inducing love to me on my wedding day,' said Vicky helpfully.

'Ah, yes, so I was. Well, then…' His thumb started to tease her nipple, sending weakness and desire dissolving through her. 'Let's continue, shall we?'

'Yes,' said Vicky faintly, as her body turned boneless, 'let's.'

BILLI⬢NAIRES' BRIDES

Pregnant by their princes...

Take three incredibly wealthy European princes
and match them with three beautiful, spirited women.
Add large helpings of intense emotion and passionate
attraction. Result: three unexpected pregnancies...and
three possible princesses—if those princes have their way.

THE ITALIAN PRINCE'S PREGNANT BRIDE
by Sandra Marton

It was payday for international tycoon Prince Nicolo Barbieri.
But he wasn't expecting what would come with his
latest acquisition: Aimee Black—who, it seemed,
was pregnant with Nicolo's baby!

Available in August.

Also available from this miniseries;

THE GREEK PRINCE'S CHOSEN WIFE
September

THE SPANISH PRINCE'S VIRGIN BRIDE
October

www.eHarlequin.com   HP12652

REQUEST YOUR
FREE BOOKS!

 HARLEQUIN *Presents*

 *PASSION GUARANTEED SEDUCTION*

2 FREE NOVELS
PLUS 2
FREE GIFTS!

YES! Please send me 2 FREE Harlequin Presents® novels and my 2 FREE gifts. After receiving them, if I don't wish to receive any more books, I can return the shipping statement marked "cancel." If I don't cancel, I will receive 6 brand-new novels every month and be billed just $3.80 per book in the U.S., or $4.47 per book in Canada, plus 25¢ shipping and handling per book and applicable taxes, if any*. That's a savings of close to 15% off the cover price! I understand that accepting the 2 free books and gifts places me under no obligation to buy anything. I can always return a shipment and cancel at any time. Even if I never buy another book from Harlequin, the two free books and gifts are mine to keep forever.

106 HDN EEXK   306 HDN EEXV

Name	(PLEASE PRINT)
Address	Apt. #
City	State/Prov.	Zip/Postal Code

Signature (if under 18, a parent or guardian must sign)

Mail to the **Harlequin Reader Service®**:
IN U.S.A.: P.O. Box 1867, Buffalo, NY 14240-1867
IN CANADA: P.O. Box 609, Fort Erie, Ontario L2A 5X3

Not valid to current Harlequin Presents subscribers.

**Want to try two free books from another line?
Call 1-800-873-8635 or visit www.morefreebooks.com.**

* Terms and prices subject to change without notice. NY residents add applicable sales tax. Canadian residents will be charged applicable provincial taxes and GST. This offer is limited to one order per household. All orders subject to approval. Credit or debit balances in a customer's account(s) may be offset by any other outstanding balance owed by or to the customer. Please allow 4 to 6 weeks for delivery.

Your Privacy: Harlequin is committed to protecting your privacy. Our Privacy Policy is available online at www.eHarlequin.com or upon request from the Reader Service. From time to time we make our lists of customers available to reputable firms who may have a product or service of interest to you. If you would prefer we not share your name and address, please check here. ☐

HP07

HARLEQUIN®

Mediterranean
NIGHTS™

Glamour, elegance, mystery and revenge
aboard the high seas...

Coming in August 2007...

THE TYCOON'S SON

by
award-winning author
Cindy Kirk

Businessman Theo Catomeris's long-estranged
father is determined to reconnect with his son, so
he hires Trish Melrose to persuade Theo to renew
his contract with Liberty Line. Sailing aboard the
luxurious *Alexandra's Dream* is a rare opportunity for
the single mom to mix business and pleasure. But
an undeniable attraction between Trish and Theo is
distracting her from the task at hand....

HM38962

Always passionate, always proud.

**The richest royal family in the world—
a family united by blood and passion,
torn apart by deceit and desire.**

By royal decree, Harlequin Presents is delighted to bring
you *The Royal House of Niroli.* Step into the glamorous,
enticing world of the Nirolian Royal Family. As the king
ails, he must find an heir...each month an exciting new
installment follows the epic search for the true Nirolian
king. Eight heirs, eight romances, eight fantastic stories!

Be sure not to miss any of the passion!

Coming in August:

SURGEON PRINCE,
ORDINARY WIFE
by Melanie Milburne

When brilliant surgeon Dr. Alex Hunter discovers he's the missing
Prince of Niroli long thought dead, he is torn between duty and
his passion for Amelia Vialli, who can never be his queen....

Coming in September:

BOUGHT BY THE BILLIONAIRE PRINCE
by Carol Marinelli

www.eHarlequin.com   HP12651